DATE DUE   MAR 0 6

5-11-06			
8-1-06			
9-12-06			
OCT 07 06			
12-5-06			
GAYLORD			PRINTED IN U.S.A.

Night Falls
Like Silk

**Center Point
Large Print**

**This Large Print Book carries the
Seal of Approval of N.A.V.H.**

KATHLEEN EAGLE

Night Falls Like Silk

CENTER POINT PUBLISHING
THORNDIKE, MAINE

For Lucia Macro,
who has always been a joy
to work with.

Remembering Oliver,
the spirit of Tommy T.

This Center Point Large Print edition
is published in the year 2004 by arrangement with
William Morrow, an imprint of HarperCollins Publishers.

The text of this Large Print edition is unabridged. In other
aspects, this book may vary from the original edition. Printed in
Thailand. Set in 16-point Times New Roman type by
Bill Coskrey and Gary Socquet.

ISBN 1-58547-390-1

Library of Congress Cataloging-in-Publication Data

Eagle, Kathleen.
    Night falls like silk / Kathleen Eagle.--Center Point large print ed.
        p. cm.
    ISBN 1-58547-390-1 (lib. bdg. : alk. paper)
    1. Comic books, strips, etc.--Authorship--Fiction. 2. Narcotic addicts--Fiction. 3. Indian
artists--Fiction. 4. Art thefts--Fiction. 5. Brothers--Fiction. 6. Large type books. I. Title.

PS3555.A385N54 2003b
813'.54--dc22
                                                                            2003017420

VICTORY HAS A HARD HEART. HARD-TO-GET by nature, she never plays games.

Hard edge notwithstanding, she had slim, sleek ankles and a great rack. Her creator was especially fond of drawing her ankles, but his own heart never failed to soften over the mouth-watering underpinnings that gave shape to her silk blouse. He went soft where she was soft, hard where she was hard, slim, and sleek.

He made her more by feel than by sight, sculpting rather than sketching her form on paper. It was the only way he could do her right. If he allowed himself to eye-ball her, she would come to him in perfect proportion— aristocratic head centered over four fine quadrants, each bearing a sturdy limb—but she would be lifeless. She would refuse to speak to him, which was her way of letting him know that he had screwed up.

Thomas Warrior depended on his creations to talk back to him. He worked in the solitude of his loft in the four-story warehouse he had saved from demolition and remodeled to suit his needs. A charter school program leased the first floor of the building for the cost of their utilities. The program's success rate with "at risk" students—a label Thomas Warrior had sported with a swagger in his days as Tommy T—was about to force him to keep a promise he almost wished he hadn't made, which involved the second floor. He enjoyed having a nice, fat cushion between his world and theirs. His world was perfect. Theirs was flawed. If they wanted a perfect world, they would have to make themselves one.

Making a perfect, self-contained world peopled with characters that could be trusted to do what they were supposed to do was, God knew, not an easy job. Thomas had found what worked for him, and he didn't want anybody messing with his creative process. As long as he kept it to himself, within the walls of his home, it was a living thing. He went out, but no one came in. No cynics, no critics, no nonbelievers infected his world or affected his illustrated adventures. His capers and those of his creations were safe in the making.

As was their discourse.

"How valuable is this thing you want rescued?" Victory asked him as she twisted the stiffness out of the neck he'd just given her.

"It's priceless to us. I'm sure its so-called owner has it insured for a price that means something to him."

"Will he collect?"

"If the insurance company is satisfied that it was stolen."

"And will they be?"

"No, of course not." Thomas had modeled the story's smug collector of Indian artifacts after his bug-eyed, thin-lipped high school geometry teacher. He'd learned a lot from Mr. Lester, felt bad when he found out about the medical problem that caused the bulging eyes, but, damn, the man had a great cartoon face. "There will be no evidence to prove that the story robe ever resided there. No photographs, no receipts, nothing but his word. Can you manage that?"

"Can Victor manage that?"

6

Ah, Victor. Thomas began the transformation.

Victor plays games. He is Victory's masculine side, her reckless, less prudent part. As Victor she will do what she must do to achieve her fleeting essence. In Victory, the man, Victor, finds the fulfillment he must seek again and again.

You never knew about Victor. Sometimes he painted his face before he went out at night, using charcoal from Victory's hearth for the left side, red clay for the right side. He was both black and red, and he liked to think he was earth and fire. But you never knew about Victor.

Thomas smiled as his beloved double-sided character came to life with the stroke of his pen.

"We'll see."

chapter 1

CASSANDRA WESTBROOK LANGUIDLY LIFTED her paddle for the man with the silky voice. The ornate fireplace poker was an unusual selection for her, but it was listed in the catalog as mid-eighteenth century, a gift from the ambassador of Sweden to railroad baron J. P. Hill. One could always use another poker.

It was a good thing the item she sought this trip was finally coming to the auction floor. She had started bidding on other items out of boredom, which could lead to mistakes. Cassandra seldom made a bad art or antique purchase unless she was bored.

It was the set of century-old Native American ledger drawings that had caught her eye in the Sotheby's of Chicago catalog. Primitives fascinated her. She loved knowing that the piece had been part of an ordinary person's everyday life in a world that to her would be, if she could drop in on it somehow, anything but everyday. Ledger drawings were particularly interesting. They were made during a transition period for Native Americans. The buffalo hides they had used to record their pictographic histories had become so scarce that they were forced to use ledger paper, often given them by their agency supervisors or their army jailors. No matter how bad conditions were, there were memories to be recorded, stories that had to be told.

A man named White Bull had made the drawings. Cassandra had no idea who he was, but his figures were especially strong in character and color, and the pages had been beautifully preserved. She expected to pay a high price. The initial barrage of bids soon became a four-way volley. When it came down to two, she permitted herself a glance in the direction of the auctioneer's polished gesture. A handsome black man accepted the challenge with a nod. He was simply dressed—black dress shirt, black slacks—and neatly groomed, but that was all she could tell about him. No jewelry, no flash, no sense of urgency or desire. Cool simplicity underscored his masculine beauty. She couldn't guess how old he was or where he came from, what language he spoke, or why he would want the drawings she now thought of as hers.

It was Cassandra's turn to bid. She nodded. This time when she glanced askance, she caught him looking at her. He didn't seem to mind being caught or being contested. His dark eyes did not hint at how far he would go, betrayed neither competitive passion nor resentment. She couldn't guess what his impressions were of her, or whether he cared what she thought of him, or what his next move might be.

"To you, sir."

He appeared not to hear the auctioneer.

"Sir?"

Cassandra lifted one eyebrow. *Will you?*

He prolonged the wait a moment longer, somehow fixing Cassandra so that she couldn't breathe, couldn't move until he did. Finally, he turned from her. With a slight shake of his head he put an end to it.

The ledger art was hers.

She wanted to speak to him, but not there in that airless, windowless room with crystal sconces and opulent chandeliers. When he left, she followed his lead, but not his path. She told herself that she would not chase him down. Her pace was leisurely; she stopped in the office to drop off her check, giving the man time to take his leave completely if that was his intention.

But he stood near a huge bronze cougar, which was perched on a pedestal for display in the huger foyer. He was watching her. She greeted one of the auctioneers, who congratulated her on her latest acquisition and asked about her plans for it. She gave a vague answer, as much for her unsuccessful competitor's benefit as for the auctioneer's. If he waited for her, planning to make her an offer, he would soon find out that he had nothing she wanted more than those drawings. Oh, she would take a congratulatory handshake, and, yes, she wanted his name. But the drawings would still be hers.

His stare seemed to heat up, as though he'd just read her thoughts and didn't much like them. It occurred to her that perhaps she should turn and walk the other way, go back to the auction even though she'd already settled her account. Handsome as he was, he had an unsettling way about him. But she decided to be the courteous winner.

"That was quite a bidding war we had going," she said. "Thank you for not running it up any higher. I was prepared to pay much more."

"I could see that. That's when I came to my senses."

She offered a pleasant smile. "And allowed the more foolish bidder to win?"

"I wouldn't say that. It's a nice set of drawings. Some people would say you got more than your money's worth." His smile chilled her. "But I doubt if those people would be anybody you'd know."

"I know a lot of people."

"Now, that's something I don't doubt." He shoved his hands into his pockets. No name. No handshake.

"I came down for this auction just for the ledger drawings. I wasn't about to let anyone else get them."

"Came down from where? Cloud or perch?"

"What would you call Minneapolis?"

"Home," he said.

"Ah, well," she enthused, refusing to let him get away without warming up to her, at least a little. "Maybe we're neighbors, in which case you're welcome to come over and visit the drawings."

"I just might do that. Did you buy them for display in your home?"

"I haven't decided. I bought them because they spoke to me."

"That's interesting," he allowed. "They speak to me, too. They speak of those people I mentioned and of their ancestors."

"The Lakota, yes. Such a fascinating people. Maybe it's no coincidence, we two Minnesotans bumping into each other in Chicago."

"Not if we're hearing the same voices. Do they tell you that they want to go home?"

"The drawings?" She glanced away, wishing she hadn't tossed out that silly cliché. Now she was forced to go shallow with the next answer, too. "Yes, they do. They want to go home with me." *Would another smile help?* "I'm not going to apologize for outbidding you, but I'm sorry for your disappointment."

He shrugged. "You win some, you lose some."

She handed him her business card. "I own a gallery in Minneapolis. I hope you'll stop in sometime."

"I'll do that. You take good care of those drawings."

"They're safe with me."

He gave a farewell gesture with her card before tucking it in his pocket.

Safe was a relative term. Stroking the cool bronze back of the cougar, he watched the woman hurry off to collect her plunder, clearly certain that she had bought and paid for the last word. Those old drawings would not reside quietly on her walls. He had given the bidding game a fair shot, but he wasn't really disappointed by the outcome.

If he knew his Victory, she would not be denied.

elsewhere

HE WAS LIKE A CAT, GLIDING AROUND through narrow spaces as though darkness didn't faze him. He was like a squirrel, storing the day's pickings in a safe place. He was like a dog, eager to please the only person in the world who mattered to him, and that person was not himself.

But he looked and felt and lived like no other creature. He looked like someone who had never been nourished. He felt like a dirty, desiccated, and scaly beast. He lived like a mole. He was less beautiful than any of the beings he identified with, but if beauty existed in the eye of the beholder, his appearance didn't matter, for no one that mattered would ever again behold him.

He called himself Victor. He lived for Victory, but he could never walk in her company, never touch her, never know her except as her contrary. His single saving grace was the belief that without him, she could not exist in the real world, or in any other. Victory was not human, but Victor was. If there were spoils, he would answer for them.

This time the spoils were the legacy of a nation. They were beautiful old things that had been bought with money and power and added to a collection. As soon as Victor had received Thomas's message, he had gone in search of the items in Thomas's book. The first step was to locate them and determine the best way to remove them from captivity. Tonight the first one had been found and reclaimed.

He had located a wooden crate, which he hoped would be a proper container for the robe. He had read up on the preservation of artifacts and did his best to do right by them in his dark sanctuary. Before laying the story robe in the paper nest he'd prepared within the box, he draped it around his shoulders, tanned side out as the old ones had worn it. It made him feel fine, almost regal. Hearing the drums inside his head, he practiced the traditional dance steps he had learned in another place and time, and for a few moments he drifted, suspended above himself, occupying a skin other than his own.

Too soon the drummers set their padded beaters aside. They took up skull-cracking war clubs and started in on the reconstruction of the interior of his head. He began to sweat.

"Damn this hide," he whispered, and he threw it off. Loath to touch the shoulders of Victory's contrary, the beautiful robe had scorched his body. He stuffed it into the box and closed the lid.

"Damn *my* hide."

Burning and aching all over, he crawled down the steps and out the door, plying the back streets of the city in search of medicine.

chapter 2

THINGS HAD CHANGED SINCE TOM HAD last been to the house on Colfax, located in the updated middle-class Minneapolis neighborhood where he had lived with Jesse and Angela Brown Wolf. The living room had gone wild. The comfortable old blue sofa was gone, replaced by a smaller tan model, which was loaded with animal-print pillows and surrounded by Angela's never-ending jungle of houseplants. Somebody had skinned an acrylic zebra and made a rug out of its hide. Glass tabletops had replaced the restored, but still kid-friendly flea market finds that had held up just fine under small hands and big feet.

The old school pictures, stationed on the bookshelves he had helped to build, had new frames. She should have gotten rid of those bookshelves along with the rest of the old furniture, he thought. There were a lot of flaws in those things—gouges from his hammer and puttied-up screw holes where he hadn't measured right. They were the kind of mistakes a guy was supposed to learn from but didn't want to see on display for the rest of his life.

"Tommy T!" His mother came charging at him like the Little Engine That Could—big round eyes, hopeful little smile. "Oh, sweetie, it's so good to see you. I didn't even hear you come in." She threw her arms around his neck. "You crept up on me."

"I don't creep, Angela. You're thinking of somebody else." He felt her go rigid in his embrace. "I still have a key to your front door. Do you want it back?"

"It's your key and always will be." She pulled back, warning, "If I don't get to mention him *my* way, the same goes for you. That's our deal."

"One question. Is he here?" He glanced past her, toward the kitchen. The first thing her husband usually did when he walked in the door was put on a pot of coffee. "This isn't another one of those accidental run-ins you've arranged, is it?"

"I won't do that again after the way you behaved the last time. I love you both too much to watch you hurt each other the way you do."

"He doesn't hurt me, Angela," he assured her as he tried out one of the new chairs. He looked up and shook his head. "It was my brother he shafted, remember?"

"He tried to help him, Tommy T." She perched on the front edge of the sofa, leaning in his direction, as though putting everything she had into her defense would help him see the man her way. "Jesse did everything he could do for Stoner."

"His name's Stony. And I'm Thomas Warrior. Not Little Warrior. Not Brown Wolf. Thomas Warrior. In my culture . . ." He glanced at the display of photographs. With a white mother and a Lakota father, the Brown Wolf clan was quite a racial hodgepodge, but he was the only one who could claim an African-American side. "In all of my cultures, people put great store by names. And I'm not crazy little Tommy T anymore."

"Not even a little bit?"

"Even my inner child has grown up."

Her doting smile nearly melted him. "Says my son the cartoonist."

Adopted son, he was tempted to remind her. But he couldn't. He'd had two real mothers. One had given him birth and the other had given him life. As for fathers, there had been one he'd hardly known, and another who had taught him all about the differences between men and heroes.

"Haven't you heard?" He tossed his soon-to-be-released graphic novel on the coffee table. "I'm a novelist. If I'd stayed with the comic books, they'd have the rights to all my characters, not just Tommy T's Dark Dog and his pack of coyotes."

"I love Dark Dog."

"I know you do. You were always way too good for him. I know his dark side better than you do," he reminded her. Jesse Brown Wolf had inspired his first comic book superhero. For Tommy T, Jesse, the tortured man he'd found hiding in a hole in the ground, had been the ever-popular Everyman by day, Supersavior by night. But once the former cop had returned to his old occupation, he'd turned out to be just another cop.

"It doesn't matter," Tom said with a lopsided shrug. "KG Comics owns Dark Dog lock, stock, and coyote hide. And I've got an agent who's making sure I never get taken like that again. I told you about the new movie deal, didn't I?"

"The sequel to *Night Thunder*?"

"We don't have a title yet," he told her, basking in the light in her eyes, the pride she took in his achievements. "But this one has to be more sophisticated. Graphic novels are working their way into a broader market, especially with the movie rights selling like cold beer at a ball game." He punched a fist into his palm. "I made them so much fuckin' cash on the last one, they had to—"

"Tom," she admonished predictably. "Please leave that language on the drawing board."

"Or out on the street? That's what you used to say." He smiled sheepishly. She'd been worse off than he was when they'd first met, but he'd never said as much. "It wasn't all bad, you know. I learned a lot. A part of me still lives there."

"It still lives in you, and it always will."

"And it made me a better person," he recited from what he fondly regarded as Angela's cherished collection of urban myths, one character after another self-combusting, only to rise from the ashes of adversity and become a teacher or an artist. Or a two-faced cop.

"You're a person still in the making," she said. "There's always room for growth and . . ."

"And what?" He glanced at the stairs. "Come on, he's not here, is he?"

"Oh, for Pete's sake, *Thomas Warrior.*" She spat out the name like it was a joke. Some pseudonym invented for his brand of fiction. "No, he's not here, and I don't expect him anytime soon. But I'm not about to plan my life around this grudge you're holding on to. I asked you to come over because I want you to meet somebody."

"A girl?" He sat back, smiling at her. The woman would not give up. "I have no trouble finding a date when I want one. Or when I need one." She questioned the difference with an arched eyebrow, and he laughed. "Either way, I don't wanna meet any more of your student teachers or the girl whose mother belongs to your book discussion group. I like *women.*"

"The person I want you to meet is a woman. She's a friend of mine and hardly a dating prospect for you."

"I get it." He wagged a finger at her. "Reverse psychology, right?"

"Her nephew is in our program."

Her school wasn't a school. It was a *program.* And he knew exactly what she would say next.

"He reminds me a lot of you."

"And who's the aunt going to remind me of?"

"Nobody. This has nothing to do with his relatives. If I could get you to mentor one child, just one, it would be Aaron. He is so talented, so bright, and so much—"

"I've told you, Angela, I don't have time." Tom slapped his hands on his knees. For him, it was case closed.

But not for Angela.

"You had an artist mentor."

"Yeah, I had two of them. One was okay, but he said

19

himself I was already a much better artist than he was. The other guy was downright weird."

"It's not about . . ." She scowled, a little slow on the uptake. "What do you mean, weird?"

"Didn't I tell you about the time he took me to the art institute and then suggested we go to his place and practice our life drawing?" He enjoyed seeing horror overtake the serene earth-mother look. He cautioned her with his own knowing smile. "And you wanted me to go to Chicago with him."

"I didn't say I wanted you to. I said you could go if you wanted to, if it was a school-sanctioned—"

He shook his head, feigning disappointment. "The one time I wanted you to say no."

"Did . . ."

"Hell, no," he retorted quickly. *"Did I what?"*

"Did anything happen?" she asked, her soft voice a counterpoint to his.

"Yeah. I told him where he could shove the whole city of Chicago, and I took a bus home from the museum. I figured I'd had enough mentoring."

"You should have told us," she said sadly.

"Us? The teacher and the cop, or my . . ." Parents? He sighed. "I was never a real kid, Angela. By the time you took me in, I'd been taking care of myself too long to start having parents. I wasn't gonna tell anybody about something that creepy. I took care of it myself. I was, what? Fourteen, fifteen by then?" He chuckled humorlessly. "He *was* good at it, though. Drawing, I mean. That old perv, he actually made his living as a commercial artist. I was impressed for about two weeks, until he showed me his other side."

"Did you think they assigned him any more students?"

"Not in my school. No, I'm pretty sure his days as a mentor ended right there."

He was not, in truth, completely sure, but reasonably so at the time. Tommy T wasn't one to narc on anybody, not even a sneaky pervert. *Stay away from me, and stay clear of my 'hood,* he'd said. *Unless you want me drawing a picture for the whole city.*

"I'm so sorry," Angela was saying. "I should've known there was something wrong. I should've—"

"You should've, I should've—hell, it's ancient history now. I lived to tell the tale." He shrugged. "I had no particular desire to *re*live it, but you dragged it out of me. It's okay, though." He waved off imaginary protests. "The mentor nightmares won't last more than a week."

"It's a good program, Tommy."

"That may well be, but from my perspective, the mentoring glass is half empty."

"You'd be such an inspiration to a talented young artist. Apparently, Aaron's mother is a little on the ditzy side, and the father has been out of the picture for some time. His mother's sister is a strong supporter of our program. We depend on support from people like her." She pulled out the stops, unfairly beseeching him with one of those don't-let-me-down looks. "Actually, I'm the one who suggested an artist as a mentor for Aaron."

"You suggested me?"

"No. Well, not exactly. I haven't suggested you yet."

"I don't mind meeting your friends, as long as we

21

don't talk about what I do," he reminded her. "That's the deal. I'm not a public person."

She threw up her hands. "Here we go."

"That's the deal, Angela. I don't get out much, don't know anybody, don't have much to say." He raised his brow. "And I don't really like kids."

"You have your own school."

"I lease them some of the extra space in my building. They can stay there as long as they don't bother me."

"Do they know that the creator of Dark Dog and Victory is their landlord?"

"The kids at the school?" He laughed. "I'm known as the rare curly-haired brown bat who lives in their belfry."

"I suppose you've added a belfry to that monstrosity, too."

"That monstrosity is my home." He grinned. He liked living in a Victorian monstrosity. He'd taken it off the city's hands for a song, but he figured he'd be pouring money into it for years to come. "You realize that no one else has been up there besides you and the kids."

"Jesse would love . . ." She frowned suddenly. "What about Stony?"

"I don't know where he is," he snapped. Case *emphatically* closed.

She blinked, surprised, unaccustomed to having him give her "that tone."

He glanced away, displeased with himself. It was a tone she didn't have coming.

"This is a waste of time, Angela. I'm doing my part for inner-city kids."

"His aunt collects American Indian art."

"I thought you said the relatives had nothing to do with it."

"I was holding this little card up my sleeve. Her husband left her a fortune. She's an art dealer, but she collects primitives."

"Primitives," he echoed, measuring each syllable. "That would be—"

The front door opened. Tom squared his shoulders and shot Angela an accusatory glance. He wasn't afraid of Jesse Brown Wolf. He simply couldn't stand to look at him. He couldn't pretend otherwise, not even for Angela's sake.

"Angela?"

It was a woman's voice, followed by a woman's footsteps and the appearance of a woman who had haunted Tom since the day they'd met. Blue eyes, long dark hair, and porcelain skin—the look of money well spent.

"I'm sorry I'm late. You told me to let myself in. This must be your"—she froze, wide-eyed, as his slow smile gave his identity away—"son."

"Cassandra, this is—"

"We've met." Tom stood, chuckling. "As a matter of fact, we've already had our first fight."

chapter 3

HER SON?

The man was too exotic, too sultry, too magnetic to be any mother's son. Particularly Angela's.

23

"We've spoken, but I wouldn't say we've met," Cassandra averred as she took off her chic swing coat and hung it on a peg in the small entryway. "You didn't tell me your name."

"Thomas Warrior."

She glanced at Angela, who explained, "Tom is our adopted son."

"But I know that name from somewhere. Thomas Warrior."

He didn't move. Still stinging from her victory over him at the auction, no doubt. Cassandra enjoyed the sound the heels of her pumps made as she moved across the hardwood floor. Feminine foot power, she thought, the reverberation of a confident woman. She offered him a handshake. "Cassandra Westbrook. I'm sure I didn't get your name at the auction. Where have I heard of you?"

"Obviously my mother doesn't brag on me much."

"You won't let me," Angela reminded him. "What auction?"

"We bid against each other on a fabulous set of Lakota ledger drawings at Sotheby's in Chicago a couple of weeks ago," Cassandra explained, acknowledging Thomas with a nod. "You were such a gentleman for dropping out before I reached the moon. Which I would have done; I was all set to go full tilt."

"Your full tilt was yet to come? I'm sorry I didn't hang a little longer, just for the ride."

Angela pointedly cleared her throat. "Well, what a coinci—"

"I might have dropped it on you," Cassandra said,

ignoring all things motherly for the moment.

"Not a chance. Not in the throes of tendering your offers"—he gave her a wink and a bit of a wicked smile—"full tilt."

"That must have been some auction," Angela muttered. "I have iced tea in the fridge. What can I offer—"

"Water would be wonderful, thanks." Any brand they had on hand would do, Cassandra told herself. "I didn't realize you were Native American," she told Thomas. "Are you and Jesse members of the same—"

"I'm a breed unto myself, as you probably noticed. My father, whom I barely remember, was black. My birth mother was Lakota. She left my world just as Angela arrived. It took two mothers to raise me."

"Between them, it appears they did a bang-up job." She folded her arms and stared, trying to put the name and the face into some context. "So, tell me. Where have I heard the name Thomas Warrior?"

"If I start guessing, I'll be giving away all my hangouts." He nodded in Angela's direction. "Watch this one, now. She's really pretending not to listen."

"I'm not interested in where you hang out," Angela demurred. "You're almost thirty years old."

"As far as you know," he told his mother. "Let's go see what she's got for us in the kitchen," he suggested to Cassandra as he led the way. "Angela tells me you have an amazing collection."

"Did I say amazing?" asked Angela, bringing up the rear. "I haven't seen it myself."

"You said 'primitives,' which, to me, is amazing." Tom took three large tumblers from the cupboard and filled them with ice as he spoke. "That generally translates to mean personal or private rather than something that was made for sale. It was usually made for the home, or maybe for a family member. Those White Bull ledger drawings are like family stories, community history." He found a pitcher of tea in the refrigerator. "The art world calls them 'primitives,' claims ownership and sells them at auction."

"They came from an estate sale." Cassandra claimed a chair at the kitchen table, mostly to get out of the way. "Maybe they were a gift from the artist. Often they were traded for something the artist needed."

"Freedom? They were often done by prisoners."

"As I said, I didn't realize that I was bidding against a Native American." Cassandra watched Tom prepare her glass of water from the tap. "Conservation of the old paper can be very tricky. I'm an art dealer, and I know what needs to be done. These happen to be in good shape because they were stashed away in what turned out to be just the right storage conditions. Now we'll do museum-quality mounting so that they can be displayed or stored safely. I like to think I'm helping to preserve the culture."

The possibility of tap water hadn't occurred to her.

"I did tell you that Thomas is a *professional* artist," Angela put in.

"That's right. Graphic arts major, you said." She lifted her glass, gave an apologetic smile. "I'm sorry. I'm preaching to the choir."

"I don't sing, and I generally don't stay for the sermon."

"Thomas Warrior," Cassandra exclaimed as the name finally clicked. She set her glass down carefully. "Our own local graphic *novelist*. There was an article about your work in *Minnesota Monthly*, wasn't there? I meant to look for the book. The artwork has a haunting quality about it. Or haunted. Maybe both."

"I hope so." He smiled, clearly pleased that she had made the connection on her own. "I try to give as good as I get."

"But there was no photograph of you featured in the article."

"I don't do press pictures. I don't want to spoil anybody's fantasy."

"What's to spoil? They should have put your face on the cover." She, too, gave as good as she got, and frankness ruled. She steepled her French-manicured fingers above the unholy tap water. "Now, tell me just what Angela has told you about my nephew."

"That he's a smart kid who likes to draw," he said with a shrug. He slid his mother a conspirator's smile. "She won't give up on getting me into this mentoring thing. She's afraid I'm becoming a recluse, which for her is anybody who doesn't have a bunch of kids around him all the time."

"Your work requires some measure of solitude," Cassandra said.

"You got it."

"So have you, Tommy," Angela said. "You have plenty of solitude. I just know that you and Aaron would hit it off famously, and you'd both—"

"I'm already hitting it off famously." He gave an open-handed gesture. "The art dealer recognized my name."

"You have so much to give, Tom," Angela cajoled. "If you'd just try it."

"I'm glad you're teaching at a private school in a safe part of town now, but if I wanted to volunteer my time at a school . . ." He glanced pointedly at Cassandra's rings and smiled when she checked to see which ones they were. "My guess is that Aaron already has all the advantages that money can buy," he said with a chuckle.

"My sister isn't—"

"Our program doesn't discriminate," Angela reminded him. "These are truly gifted children from all over the city. Once a child is accepted, he receives the best we have to offer, whether he has community sponsorship or his parents are able to pay his tuition." To her credit, Angela's pitch sounded fresh, even though this was evidently not the first time Thomas had heard it. "In my judgment, this would be a good fit for both of you. Aaron could use a strong male influence in his life, and you . . ." She smiled gently. "Well, Thomas Warrior, you need to get over yourself just a bit. You'd really be very good for each other, I think."

With a chuckle, Thomas leaned toward Cassandra, aping an aside. "Angela will never stop trying to fix me up. I'd be careful if I were you."

"Careful for . . ."

"When she finds me 'a good fit,' I never know what to expect."

"I'm talking about Aaron," Angela said.

"And you let this woman teach your nephew?" Thomas teased.

"Listen, you're obviously unavailable for—"

The back door burst open at the hand of Angela's youngest child, eleven-year-old Sam. "Tommy T!" he shouted. "When did you get here? I didn't know you were coming over."

"Hey, bro," Thomas said, opening himself up for a hug.

But Sam had a manlier greeting in mind. "Hey, man, how's it goin'?"

Thomas shifted smoothly into the latest homeboy handshake. "Where's the ol' man?"

"He's out in the garage. He'll be stoked when he finds out who's here. You never—"

"I just stopped in. You doin' okay? School's goin' okay?"

"It's all right, I guess. When can I come over? You never let me stay at your place anymore. It's been months since I got to stay over for a weekend, or even one night."

"We'll do something next week, okay? I promise."

Thomas turned as the door was opened without clamor this time. He drew a deep breath, releasing it on a smile for his sister, fifteen-year-old Serena, whom Angela and Jesse had adopted as a baby within months of his own adoption.

"Hey, Squeakers." He stood quickly. This one wasn't getting past him without a hug.

"Stop calling me that, Tommy T!"

"Yeah, well, don't *you* call me *that*. You just ruined me." He leaned back to get a better look at the top and jeans that bared a considerable expanse of the pretty blonde's midriff. "Angela, this shirt she's wearing, this is *not* a good fit."

"Cut it out." Serena plucked at a button on Thomas's black dress shirt. "What do you know about clothes? You've gone totally *GQ*."

"That's cold, woman."

"But true." Serena grabbed her big brother's forearm as a warning clatter sounded in the garage, on the other side of the back door. "Don't fight with Dad, okay?"

"What, fight? We don't fight."

"You do when you talk."

"That's why we don't talk." He turned to Cassandra. "I'll meet with your nephew, and we'll see what we can work out."

"Wonderful. You'll schedule it with Angela, then?"

He shook his head. "With you. Have his mom bring him over to your place, and I'll be there. We'll see if we have any chemistry."

"You and Aaron," Cassandra reflected.

"Or maybe me and your sister, who knows? Can you arrange it?" He bent to kiss Angela's cheek. "I've got a deadline, Mom."

Still seated at the table, Angela grabbed Tom's hand. "Stay a little and just say hello to him. He misses you so much."

"I've got things to do."

"Too late," Serena whispered as Jesse Brown Wolf came through the back door.

He was a man whose cares showed in his face even when they were at rest in him. He saw Cassandra immediately and offered the kind of smile that made a

30

woman's heart swell. "Hey, we've got company."

"You remember Cassandra," Angela contributed. "She's—"

The small kitchen felt like a packed elevator as anxiety welled up in all the empty space.

The warning buzzer went off when Jesse's eyes met Tom's. Jesse's smile dissolved mid-handshake with Cassandra. She might have been shaking hands with a piece of wood.

"Good to see you," he told her, but there was no indication that he remembered her or that he actually saw her. He was edgy, eager to speak to his son.

The two men exchanged brief nods. It might have been a chance encounter in occupied territory between two big dogs, circling, each waiting for the other to make the first sound.

But they were not dogs. They were men who shared a level of emotion that might have choked them had they been women. Cassandra could almost see it, bobbing in their throats. She knew little of their history, but the heat they generated made her wonder whether Aaron really needed a male role model.

The dogged stubbornness of youth prevailed.

"It's good to see you, son." Tentatively, Jesse offered his hand. Tom studied it for a moment, as though shaking hands—shaking this particular hand—might change the course of his life. He raised his eyes slowly to meet those of the man who had adopted him at the age of thirteen and changed both their lives.

Hope met rejection, and finally sadness mirrored sadness.

"I came to see Angela. She called me."

Jesse withdrew his hand. "It's good to see you're still alive," he tossed off lightly as he stepped back over some invisible line they'd tacitly established between them.

"Yeah," Tom said with a shrug. "You, too." He turned to Angela. "I gotta be going. Tell Cassandra how she can get in touch with me." And to Cassandra he offered a "later" gesture. "You give me a call after you've talked it over with the boy. We'll set something up."

Cassandra barely had time to nod before he was gone. It felt like watching a storm pass.

Although his face betrayed little emotion, the way Jesse Brown Wolf spoke and moved and drifted in and out of what remained of the conversation silently reaffirmed the brief acknowledgment of loss that had passed between him and his son. Clearly they'd been close once.

It was equally clear to Cassandra—if not to anyone else in the room—that Angela was eager to explain.

Sam and Serena politely took their leave. As soon as Jesse excused himself, Angela leaned in for a tête-à-tête with Cassandra. She realized then, for the first time, that Angela trusted her as a friend.

"Tom's older brother ended up in prison after Jesse arrested him in a drug bust," Angela revealed quietly. "That was four years ago. Tom never understood how hard it was for Jesse. Jesse knew Stony would be arrested that night, and he didn't have to be there. It was his way of making sure that Stony wasn't harmed. At that point it was the best he could do. Stony had stayed with us for a while, off and on, in and out of rehab, but he just couldn't . . ." She drew a deep, unsteady breath, pressed her lips together, and shook her head. "Stony couldn't stay away from his old stomping grounds."

Cassandra didn't know what to say. She thought about her sister, Darcy, who had tried every mischief known to man when they were growing up, and she thought about Darcy's son, who was the moodiest twelve-year-old she'd ever met. Not that she'd met many. She felt an obligation to do what she could for what little family she had.

"That's quite a challenge, taking in kids like that."

"I can't do it anymore. Jesse won't let me," Angela whispered. "He says he won't let me because he knows I feel bad, saying I can't do it anymore."

"Personally, I really appreciate your current mission. My nephew is a challenge, too, and my sister isn't really stepping up to the plate. She's sort of a free spirit. I love them both—they're all I have, really—but I'm not sure how far I should go, whether I'm interfering when I make a suggestion or offer to foot the bill for something I think might help. Like school tuition." Cassandra sighed, secretly glad her worry was comparatively small. Kids outgrew moodiness. "It's not like he's my own child. He has a mother."

"Tommy T was my first child, and he was twelve going on twenty when I met him." Angela gave a small laugh. "You didn't hear me call him Tommy T," she warned before sliding down her own memory lane. "I said we took him in. Before that, he took me in—into his city. I was running away." She grimaced, slipping Cassandra a secret look. "From a man, can you believe? I got in the car and drove until I thought I'd reached a place where no one would ever find me. Tommy T helped me find a job, and I gave him a place to sleep. Now he's twenty-nine, going on forty. He picked up a few years when he had to identify his mother's body after a hit-and-run, another couple when his brother went to prison."

"Where does he live?"

"I'm not sure."

Not sure? Maybe Cassandra wasn't such a trusted friend.

"I know his address," Angela hastened to add, "but I'm not sure how much of him lives there. He makes his living creating a fantasy world, and I think that's where he spends most of his time these days. I know his success has made him more distant. I was hoping . . ."

"He said we'd set something up. That sounds positive. Just meeting him would be fun for Aaron, and I'd love to see his work."

"No one sees his work in progress. No one gets into his studio. I can't even tell you where he lives. I'm sworn to secrecy."

Cassandra laughed. "Ah, the eccentric artist. My favorite brand. He'll be quite nonplussed when he finds out how well I know him."

"Don't be too sure. Tommy T was always full of surprises. Thomas Warrior has turned them into secrets."

"Either way, I'm sure I know him."

chapter 4

VICTORY TOOK SHAPE BENEATH THOMAS
Warrior's hand. She pushed him to draw faster, impatient
with his dawdling fingers. But he couldn't decide where
to put her.

He was running out of story. He needed a new source
of trouble, a new threat to Victory's rejuvenation in
places and among people who had never seen her for
themselves and found her hard to imagine, but who still
believed.

Not that people like that existed in the real world, but
real-world readers of all ages continued to pay the cover
price of getting off on the heroic fantasy.

Tom had been a believer once. He couldn't remember
a time when he wasn't drawing something from his fantasy world, coming up with characters who could go
anywhere, do anything, save lives or find a treasure in
the last place an ordinary person would expect to
encounter something of value. He had believed with
such intensity that he had coaxed a man up and away
from the grave of his own making.

One would hope Jesse Brown Wolf might have
returned the favor.

One *what* would hope?

One kid. One ragtag boy who used his fantasies to
make his world bearable. A kid should be allowed hope.

But a man who made his living creating fantasy
should have known better. When push came to shove,
Jesse the champion of children gave no more than a fee-

ble push against Jesse the cop's inevitable shove. Either of the two Jesses could have found a way to spare Stony, to bail him out, give him one more chance. Stony was never a threat to anybody but himself. He was like their mother—always in the wrong place at the wrong time making the wrong move.

Tom hadn't heard from his brother since he'd gotten out of the pen. No phone call for a ride or a place to stay or a few bucks to get him by until the job he was promised came through. Maybe no news was good news. Tom couldn't blame Stony for not trusting him, but it would be nice to know he was okay.

Oddly, the ringing phone startled him. He thought he'd turned the ringer off. Anyone who had been entrusted with the number knew better than to call him early in the morning unless they simply wanted to leave a message. If the work had been going well, he'd be asleep by now, and if it wasn't, he wouldn't be somebody they'd want to bother.

By the second ring something told him he didn't want to miss this call.

"What's up?"

"Frankly, I wasn't going to call." The rich, refined voice called red-brown hair and exhilarating blue eyes to his mind. "You didn't really seem interested," she said, "and I really don't want to impose."

"I'm very interested. Don't worry about imposing."

"That's very nice of you, Thomas, but I got the distinct impression that you were being pushed in a direction you really have no interest in—"

"Angela knows she can't push me," he told her.

He glanced at the one timepiece in the loft—a workers' time clock from one of the old flour mills that fit his eclectic décor and served as a cautionary piece—and he realized just how early it was. Another cautionary piece, no doubt from the gods. Here was Venus starting her day as Mars was finishing his.

But there was that lush hair, and those jewel-tone eyes, and his wish to hear her voice some more.

"I don't let anyone impose, and I'm not interested in being nice," he challenged. "What made you decide to call?"

"I said I would."

He chuckled. "Come on, say it. You're just as interested as I am."

"Do you have time for dinner this week?"

"I'll make time if you're making dinner."

"I'll have dinner here. I'm not sure who will prepare it, although I'm perfectly capable when the spirit moves me. My sister and her son will be here, too, of course."

"Of course. That's what this is about."

"And my collection of Native American art will be here, if you'd like to see it."

"Why would it be anywhere else? Does it travel?"

"Sometimes," she said, as though it were a matter of some course that he surely knew about. "When I want to make room for something new. Like the ledger drawings."

"Be careful, woman. Don't twist the knife."

"Drop in at the gallery sometime. Maybe I can interest you in something else."

He smiled at his unfinished Victory. "You already have."

She had no idea how much.

CASSANDRA OFTEN HOSTED DINNER PARTIES but she rarely invited anyone to her home simply for a quiet meal. Her sister, Darcy, might drop in once in a while, but it was never planned. As far as Cassandra knew, Darcy never made plans. She simply did whatever she felt like doing at the moment. But Darcy liked the idea of finding a mentor for Aaron. She liked the word *mentor,* which she had said sounded classier than *Big Brother,* and she was curious about any man who would volunteer for mentor duty. It all added up to a significant probability that Darcy would probably show up. Of course, if a better offer came along, she would suddenly decide she couldn't stay, but would it be all right if she picked Aaron up later that night? The next day would be even better.

Either way, Cassandra would have more than one guest for dinner. She would have a familiar role to play, which would mask the troublesome fascination Thomas Warrior suddenly held for her. She had picked up the phone at least a dozen times before finally making the call, and the sound of his voice had given her goose bumps.

There was no place in her life for goose bumps. The men in her life were either young and gay or old and rich. They were predictable. Their effect on her was exactly what she expected it to be. Widowhood, she had decided, was much underrated.

Having her psyche buffeted about by one temperamental man was enough for a lifetime. Over the last six years she had enjoyed being Edgar Westbrook's widow far more than she had being his wife, particularly in those final few years. There was no walking on eggshells, no biting her tongue, no swallowing bile or anything else that might capriciously be required. It was hard to remember the powerful, witty, sophisticated man she had married, and it was painful to recall herself as his child bride. It seemed like such an archaic arrangement to her now. But nobody could have persuaded her that there was anything wrong with a quarter-century age difference. Not then. Even now she wasn't sure that the difference in their ages had caused a problem. It was her naïveté, pure and simple.

That was Cassandra at nineteen—pure and simple.

Twenty years later, she was neither pure nor simple. The power, wit, and sophistication were all hers now, along with the house overlooking Lake of the Isles and the money. She had divested herself of all interest in Edgar's business and invested in the business that interested her.

Talented artists, living and dead, interested her. Her only talent was for studying and picking them out and appreciating them. She had met and married Edgar under circumstances that embarrassed her when she thought about them. She never talked about it, and she hoped most of the community had forgotten that she'd been a beauty pageant contestant, and that Edgar had been one of the judges. She'd been a college freshman in need of a scholarship. He'd been a pillar of the community in need of diversion. She'd been second runner-up for the crown, but first, Edgar had sworn, in his heart. He offered tuition, room and board, and an immediate MRS. She had earned her art history degree and continued to study, partly because Edgar had also chosen to put the beauty pageant history behind them. He dressed her in fine clothes, encouraged her "pursuit of class," and paraded her proudly.

There would be no children. Cassandra originally had the impression that Edgar expected them. Whenever she was ready, he'd said, but as time and the marriage wore on, having a child became one of many subjects that were never openly discussed, one of the things she often thought about or fretted over but never mentioned. Leaving well enough alone was the best way to live with Edgar. There was enough that was not well between them, and detaching herself from the *not well* required her considerable effort.

One day, out of the blue, he'd mentioned that he was sterile. He'd known it for years—more years than they'd been married—and he'd mentioned it as casually as someone might say that he was not hungry. That was the day she had begun to think about who she was, what she had, what she did day after day and night after night, and how much of it was attributable to Edgar. What did it matter that he was old enough to be her father? Until that day, the question had always been rhetorical. It was then that Cassandra had truly seen herself through her husband's eyes. For Edgar, wife and child were one and the same.

But she didn't have to worry about what it meant to be that kind of a hybrid anymore. Neither wife nor child, Cassandra was secure in her widowhood.

At the sound of the chimes, she took a deep, cleansing breath and measured an unhurried stride toward the door.

Get thee behind me, goose bumps.

"You're early." She smiled quickly, lest he take her greeting the way it sounded. "Or maybe they're late."

"In either case, you're ready." He gave the foyer a quick ceiling-to-floor survey as he stepped inside. Then he turned to her and appraised in reverse, from the hem of her long black skirt to its matching sweater, simple gold pendant, new shade of lipstick purchased earlier that day at the salon where she'd had her hair cut a week before her standing appointment turned up on her calendar.

His eyes finally met hers and hinted at a smile. "Very nice."

"Thank you." She stepped back, deeper into the security of her own ornate territory. "It's too much house for one person, but every time I think about getting something smaller—you know, simplifying—well, I can't decide what I would let go. I've been called a pack rat."

"But you're packin' only the best," he noted as he scanned the series of soft, muted watercolors flanking the arched doorway to the living room.

They were California landscapes from the 1930s, the tail end of a period in American art that was a particular favorite of hers. "Would you like to see—"

"You." He turned to her, the barest hint of a smile boosted by the warmth in his eyes. "How fine you're looking—that's what I'm talkin' about."

"Thank you," she repeated. It was heartfelt this time.

She caught a glimpse of their reflections in the console mirror, and it occurred to her that he looked better in black than she did. She would have said as much aloud, but the two people in the mirror seemed so distant and looked so completely at ease that she wondered whether someone had removed the mirror and hung an art deco poster she'd forgotten she had. They made a handsome, ageless, timeless pair. Both slender and sleek in their rich, understated variations on a black silk theme, they appeared to stand on equal footing, even though he stood half a head taller than she. His shoulders were equally square but more relaxed. His curly, close-cropped hair was darker, his skin tone richer, his profile so much more angular and interesting than hers.

It was a deceptive reflection, all right. She could have sworn he filled the space, and she was just there.

She couldn't abide being "just there." With a sweeping gesture, she took a giant sidestep. "I have some wonderful photographs in the study—original Curtises and Fiskes—and a set of ledger drawings from . . ."

His teasing smile threw her off track.

She reeled in the gesture and lifted an eyebrow. "What?"

"I'm paying you compliments, and you're all biz. Let me hear you say what I saw in your eyes when you opened the door." He spread his hands, inviting her inspection. "I dressed for the occasion, too."

"You look gorgeous, and you obviously know it."

"Man, you are one cold beauty. Now which part only goes skin-deep?" He tempered his grin with a challenge. "You're gonna let me find out for myself, right?"

"Are you always this direct?"

"Pretty much." He shoved his hands in the pockets of his neatly pressed slacks. "Maybe I should meet the family and do dinner before you show me your treasures."

"Treasures," she muttered as she led the way through the arch, grateful for the show of true male colors in a typically drab remark, easily fielded by an intelligent woman. "Some in the art world would argue that primitives are valuable only from a historical perspective, but I think some folk art transcends history and culture exactly the way fine art does. It belongs to everyone and no one, just like the work of the great masters, the classical writers and musicians."

"All I know is, my stuff belongs to whoever pays my price," he told her offhandedly. He was drawn into the living room by her contemporary Native American collection, pulled from one painting to the next.

"Your work is commercial." Expounding was what she did to make herself feel comfortable with the act of following several paces behind him. "It's quite popular, from what I understand. But you're also very good."

"What does that mean, *but* you're also very good? I can't be both commercial and good?"

"Of course you can. What I meant was that . . ."

His expectant glance drove hers away.

She spoke softly into a vase full of fresh trumpet lilies. "Just that you're very good."

"How do you know?" he wondered idly, moving on to

43

the painting that was the focal piece in the room. "You read comic books?"

"After I found out who you were, I visited several bookstores and bought everything I could find with your name on it. I like to start with an artist's early work so I can appreciate the various directions his development has taken. You're all over the map."

He chuckled. "Yeah, but I think I'm closing in on discovering my true self."

"Do you have a connection to White Bull, the ledger artist?"

"A connection?" He was absorbed in the geometric interpretation of a colorful, swirling Native dancer. Reverently he touched the signature of artist Oscar Howe. "We're all related. So says the Lakota philosopher.

"But there are all kinds of connections." He spun toward her, shoving that hand into his pocket again as though his fingertips had captured something from the painting that he could keep for himself. "You can see the old drawings in Howe's style. Time doesn't exist. It's the life and the breath and the circling of one people. Those drawings are more about the soul of a nation than its history. White Bull showed less of what *was* and more of what should have been."

"I have the same impression," she said, picking up on his fervor. "He embellishes a bit with the handful of warriors standing their ground against the multitude, but he shows a progression of events, both on the battleground and in the village, which is very interesting. The unusual detail and the way he uses color to achieve a sense of depth make the drawings so hard to resist."

"And why try? Will you be selling them anytime soon?"

"I have no plans to sell them."

"What about donating them to a museum?" he wondered.

"I'll probably put them out on loan, but not for a while. I want to—" She turned, startled by the sound of the back door opening. "Ah, they're here. Finally."

Tom smiled. *Saved by the sister*. For a moment he'd had her in the palm of his hand.

He stood awkwardly, waiting for the introductions and the small talk and the clock watching to begin. The reason she'd created for him to be there related to a short, shy kid who could have played the Pillsbury doughboy, minus the giggle and the grin. His mother, on the other hand, was all soft-spoken come-ons, shimmers, and curves.

Tom decided to give Aaron his usual benefit of the doubt for a kid who'd clearly gone out of his way to adopt a needy mother.

"So, what exactly do you do, Tom?" Darcy asked as she passed a napkin-draped basket. "Cassie says you're an artist, but most of Cassie's artists turn out to be something else besides. Bread?"

"Bread, sure. Offering or collection?" He took the basket and the blank stare, returning a smile. "I do just fine as an artist. I make plenty of bread."

Blink. Blink. Still blank.

"You want me to help myself, or kick in? I'm fine, either way."

"Thomas isn't one of *my* artists," Cassandra said, inviting him to exchange secret glances with her. *Clever-*

ness appreciated. "Not struggling, in other words."

"Congratulations on being one of the few," Darcy said. "You don't look married. Married people tend to look married, and you have a very unmarried look about you. Do you have a girlfriend? Boyfriend?"

"Friends are a lot of work," Tom quipped. "I'm completely unattached."

"Likewise. Except for Aaron, of course. Poor kid, he's surrounded by women. Mom, Aunt Cassie, teachers, even the dog."

"We don't have a dog anymore," the boy reminded her. "But you *do* have—"

"She ran away last month." Darcy grabbed her turn to slip Tom a secret, sad glance. She patted her son's arm. "It would be nice to be around a man once in a while, wouldn't it, hon?" Back to Tom, between adults. "He's always quiet when he first meets someone."

"What's your favorite medium?" Tom asked Aaron as he broke his bread.

"Pencil, but I'm getting into pen and ink. I like the way it looks, but I mess up more."

"It takes practice."

"He gets practice," Darcy interjected. "He's always drawing. He probably needs a tutor in math more than art and somebody to get him interested in some sport. You obviously work out, Tom. Maybe you could—"

"I'm not interested in tutoring or volunteering for Big Brothers or being Aaron's Uncle Tom." Thomas lowered his voice. "Do you know what mentoring is about, Aaron?"

"Kind of, yeah. Mrs. Brown Wolf said her son—well,

you, I guess, when you were my age, you had a mentor."

"Two, actually."

"Whatever. She says you gotta have the right match-up."

"She's got that right. I learned some valuable lessons working with mentors."

"About what?"

"People." Tom was buttering his bread. "That whole match-up thing, that's important. And I learned some things about going to work and about doing what you do best."

"About being an artist? Did you learn about that?"

"I already was an artist. Like you, I was always drawing, and I knew I was good at it. What I learned . . ." He set his knife down on the edge of his plate, blade out—a propriety he'd learned at Angela's table, along with being a conversational player. "I discovered that I had a long way to go to become a professional."

And a long way to go until dessert.

But go he did. He complimented Cassandra on the Cornish hen and the wild rice and answered Darcy's questions about his family and his work without getting too specific about how he fit into the picture. He didn't have to. Her interest was marginal.

Finally, Tom jumped at the opportunity to stretch his legs by suggesting that he and Aaron clear the table.

Cassandra followed, but only to retrieve a large glass bowl from the fridge. She flashed him a thumbs-up kind of smile. "Do you like trifle?"

"I can handle small servings, but we're homing in on my limit."

She laughed. "This is all I need from the kitchen. Take a break while we set up for coffee."

He took her glancing hint and turned to find Aaron hanging back at the sink and watching him in wonder. He had the look of a kid dying to say something, but it was taking him a moment to put it together.

"I've read the whole 'Dark Dog' series, so I know who you are."

"Mrs. Brown Wolf didn't tell you?"

"She said she wanted to hook me up with somebody special because of the kind of drawing I like to do." He lifted one shoulder, as though he'd been given leave to confess with no threat of penance. "I don't always do my other work. Sometimes I get ideas for stuff I want to draw when I'm supposed to be doing other stuff."

"I know how that goes," Tom sympathized. Because it was handy, he tucked a tall stool between his legs and took a seat. "I don't go around talking about my books. I keep to myself pretty much. I work better that way."

"Yeah, me, too."

Aaron edged a few inches toward the back door, as though he might take to the air.

Starting up from his own perch, Tom noticed the folder at the end of the counter near the door, and he settled back down. "I'd like to see some of your drawings. Did you bring any?"

"Not the good stuff." It was the boy who flew. He landed directly on the source of what little confidence he had. "I just brought the stuff from school."

"I know what you're saying. Some people wouldn't get it, so why show it to them?" Tom took the drawings in hand, appraising the pages one by one. He smiled at the sketch of a kid who had fallen asleep at his desk. "But this shows me that you've got a good eye."

"I've got my own characters," Aaron confided, suddenly almost breathless with excitement. "They're like different levels of human. I got the idea from the theories about how maybe the Cro-Magnons and the Neanderthals overlapped, so you had these two species with different powers, you know? And not like part human and part something else, like vampires or werewolves."

"Interesting."

"If you mentor me, I can have one whole day a week just for art."

"A whole day?" He made a mental note to call Angela.

"Not just with you," Aaron said quickly, reaffirming Tom's observation of his good eye. "You wouldn't have to be around me all day."

"You wouldn't *want* to be around me all day." Tom tucked the drawings back into the folder. "If your mom approves, should we give it a shot?"

"She approves." Aaron glanced toward the door to the dining room. "Is there any rule about mothers not going out with their kids' mentors? Because if there isn't, there should be."

"Let's make one. As long as we're working together, it's hands off your mother." They slapped hands to seal the bargain before Tom added, "But your aunt is fair game."

"Aunt Cassie? You're not her type."

"What type does she go for?"

"Rich old farts."

Tom laughed. "Oh, yeah, the snow-on-the-mountain kind who drive those long, pimpin' boats around your neighborhood."

"This isn't our neighborhood."

"This is the first time I've been here myself."

Aaron lifted one plump shoulder. "Aunt Cassie doesn't really go for those guys. She just hangs out with them because, I don't know, women need guys to go places with, I guess."

"You get along with her pretty well?"

"Oh, yeah." The boy finally managed to smile. "I think she's beautiful. Don't you?"

"As one artist to another? Like I said, I can tell you've got a good eye."

COFFEE WAS READY IN THE DINING ROOM, and with the table set for dessert, Cassandra was ready to wrap things up. Her good deed had taken on the perfect shape and was about to roll. That Thomas was taking a few minutes aside with Aaron could only be a good sign. She wasn't sure whether her warm face was a sign of anything but a warm room, but she had to open a window before she sat down with Darcy and whispered, "Well, what do you think?"

"About this guy?"

"Thomas."

"Thomas," Darcy echoed, mimicking Cassandra's instructive tone. "I think he's a hottie. I was expecting some pale, puny, sensitive type. But I gotta hand it to you, Cassie, you picked a real stud. Deliciously exotic-looking and so mysterious. Whew! I hope you can handle him."

"What are you talking about? He's going to work with Aaron, who desperately needs—"

"Oh, that part's fine, too." Darcy dismissed her sister's protest with a wave of her hand. "I agree. Aaron's becoming such a glum kid that I don't know what to do with him anymore. A shot in the arm? A kick in the pants? I don't know. Why can't he get interested in basketball? Does Tom play basketball?"

"I have no idea. We've only discussed his art and the possibility of his working with Aaron."

"Ah, but there's a conversation going on between the lines, dear sister." Darcy leaned scrunch-shouldered across the corner of the table for a tête-à-tête. "I'm very good at reading these things. Isn't it amazing how sisters can be so different? Your interest in the arts is such a contrast to my fascination with the sciences. Chemistry. Electricity. Magnetic fields. Would that be physics?"

"My foot," Cassandra muttered.

"Anatomy, yes." Darcy touched a red nail to what, before dinner, had been a bright red lip. "His age is hard to guess, but he's obviously a somewhat younger man. That's delicious, too, and not at all surprising. You're due." She wagged the lip-touching finger. "The protest is on the tip of your tongue, but you can't quite spit it out because you know how well I know you."

"I really hate that about you, Darcy." Cassandra smiled. How long had it been since she'd warmed this way to a conversation with Darcy? "I hardly know him, but I feel like I do. With most men, I know a lot about them, and it's all the same from one to the next, and I'm perfectly comfortable with that. But this man is different. I don't know much about him at all, but we have this odd familiarity thing going on. He seems to know what I'm thinking, and I know what he's thinking, and it's—"

"Chemistry, dear. Something you never had with old Edgar. My advice is to let yourself go. Have fun with it. You can afford anything you want. Why not a boy toy?"

"I don't remember asking for any advice." Cassandra scowled theatrically. As much as she wanted to object to the *boy toy* remark, she hated to shut down the rare flow of warmth between them. Anything but a teasing "I didn't, did I?" would bring on the usual chill.

"You never do. I wish you would. This is my particular area of expertise."

"My odd familiarity thing aside, how do you want to set this mentorship up?"

"What does it cost?"

"There's no fee involved, but there might be—"

"Because I'm kind of strapped, and I'm going to have to ask you for another loan."

Oh, the chill. Cassandra froze, waiting for her sister to put the point on her need. It was always a blunt one.

"I'm late again."

"Late with . . ." Cassandra closed her eyes as the cold wave rolled over her. "Damn it, Darcy, you promised me that you were going to try that birth control shot."

"I am. I was. Cassie, I *will* after this, I promise." Darcy drew a deep breath and inched her hand across the table.

Cassandra ignored it.

"I bought a pregnancy test kit. I haven't used it yet. Maybe . . ." Darcy gave a shaky sigh.

Drama queen, Cassandra shouted, but only in her head. The worst thing she could do was speak. Nothing she could say would make any difference. Just be quiet, she told herself. Inside and out.

Darcy spoke quietly. "I don't want to go through another abortion, Cassie, but I can't have another kid."

Cassandra finally lifted her gaze to meet her sister's slightly teary one. She knew the look in her own eyes was cool, but it was the best she could do.

"Say something," Darcy pleaded.

"I don't know what to say."

"Yes, you do. I'm a shitty mother."

"I wouldn't say that." Her tone had turned from teen-ish to teacher-ish. She knew it. She heard it. But it was the best she could do. "Not being a mother myself, I couldn't say that. I *can* say that you have no business getting pregnant now. And I don't think I'm being the least bit judgmental, all things considered."

"But if I am, you'll help me?"

Cassandra glanced away. *Help, help, help,* said a small voice inside her hastily built steel barricade.

"You did before," Darcy said softly.

"You've got to take better care of yourself, Darcy. I can only do so much."

"All I'm asking for is money, and it's an amount you won't miss at all."

Only money. All she needs is money, and I won't miss it.

Cassandra sat down at her desk, but she stopped short

of turning on the lamp. She could hear Aaron telling his mother that Thomas was going to help him develop his talent for drawing. "He says I've got a good eye," Aaron said with as much conviction as she'd heard in his voice in some time.

Across the hall, by the overflow of light from the dining room, Cassandra wrote out a check to her sister.

elsewhere

VICTOR WAS WORRIED. IT WAS UNLIKE Thomas to involve himself personally with someone Victor would be visiting, and the mandate for Cassandra Westbrook was clear. Thomas wisely insulated himself from mundane matters that might compromise or taint his mission. A woman could easily do both.

Victor had achieved immunity against most human needs. He took inspiration from Victory and direction from Thomas, but he sought neither love nor approval. Certainly, in this life, redemption was out of the question. But when he was gone, he wanted to be remembered for carrying out Thomas's mission, which was the honorable thing, the only truly right thing he'd ever done.

When he was gone, he would finally be visible.

He envisioned people he'd never met filing slowly past his casket, their hearts breaking as they peered into the star-quilt–draped box at the face of the man who had recovered the treasures of their ancient culture. They would speak words like *brave* and *heroic* and *unselfish*. "We've lost a fine warrior," they would say. "How will we honor him?"

Victory would stand over him. *By using what we've brought home to you to teach the children to be proud,* his spirit would tell them through her.

Words to live and cry by.

The people knew nothing of his past except that he had been born among them. It was all they needed to know. Victor imagined the people shedding a river of tears for him when he was gone—a new river that would rush from his burial hill like spring runoff, sparkling in the afternoon sun. When they tasted the water, they would find that it was pure and fresh. It would nourish the land and bring new life to the reservation. This would be the single event that Thomas had not conceived, a miracle made by the sheer power of returning to the people—even in death—with Victory.

A dream to live and die by.

Thomas's words and pictures gave Victor an identity and a mission that would bring him home to the people. He belonged to them, and he had served them well, thanks to Thomas Warrior.

And where would Thomas be? How would he feel when Victor was gone? Would Thomas replace him with another changeling like himself and continue the work with a new mission?

Or would the woman step in and fuck everything up?

No chance. Thomas was too smart to let anything so dreary and dull as a woman change the way he needed to live—the way *they* needed to be. The three of them—

Thomas, the thinker; Victor, the doer; Victory, the redeemer—together they made one being. There was no room for more.

Victor ascended the secret stairs, making his way in total darkness to the secret door. They were two of many precious secrets, entrusted to him to guard and to use as the need arose. From the secret world into the shadowy world, the gray matter of Thomas's creativity, the streaks of red blood, the warmth of organic matter—wood and wool—and the charge of electricity. Thomas lived and worked in the world above Victor's, but their worlds were connected. The opportunity to ascend and linger awhile, however, was rare.

Victor appeared and disappeared as their mission required. He took direction from the storyboards, the notes, and the colorful drawings. He listened to the tapes Thomas made. The actual tape-recording was Victor's job, a means to gather every aspect of Thomas's prized plots and plans. Nothing could be allowed to fall away unheeded.

Victor searched for hidden clues and discreet, possibly unrealized or yet-to-be-realized wishes, muted commands. But on rare occasions like this one—time and clear head permitting—he took bits of sustenance that would not be missed, lay on the big bed that would not be shared, absorbed whatever essence Thomas might have left behind, and imagined his own essence blending to the point of his own disappearance as night fell.

He was halfway there.

chapter 5

AFTER DARCY AND AARON LEFT, CASSANDRA broke out the cognac. She handed Thomas a glass, wordlessly asking him to stay a while longer.

He touched his glass to hers and knocked back the first drink. "Good stuff," he said through a grimace.

"Not 'Thanks, I needed that'?"

He gave her glass a pointed glance. "Am I the only one?"

She took a short sip, followed by a longer one. It went down warm and welcome. Strong drink was a doubt-killer, clearly a shared need. When she took their glasses back to the decanter for refills, she felt his heat at her back. His hands on her shoulders caused her to botch the second pouring.

"You've got something to show me?"

"Follow me upstairs," she said as she handed him his glass.

At the top of the landing, she took his arm and drew him to the tall leaded glass window overlooking the lake. "This is the best way to watch night fall," she said. "It's a safe vantage point. With my home all around me, I have the best the outdoors has to offer—a view."

"You saying you're not much of an outdoor girl?"

"That's what I'm saying." She sipped slowly. The drink had already settled every nerve in her body, its aftertaste lingering in her mouth like the last rosy streaks in the sky. "What about you?"

"Honey, I've lived outdoors. I like having that door to

close behind me."

"Angela hasn't told me much, but I gather she took you in . . ."

"Off the streets? It's okay. You can say it."

With night's soft settling, the city lights emerged like jewelry for the lady of the lake, whose lovers would admire her from a safe distance until morning. "What she did say was that you saved her life in more ways than one."

"She got mugged," he said. He drained his glass and set it on the window seat. "I got her some help. We got to be kind of a team after that."

"How old were you then?"

"I don't remember."

"Right." She turned to him, smiling. He stood so close that all she saw was the way the moonlight accented the fullness of his lips, and all she felt was anticipation. "Your mother and I have become friends."

"Let it go." He took her glass, set it beside his, and drew her into his arms. "Let it go, Cassandra. This is between you and me by the light of the rising moon."

Their first kiss was as silky as nightfall, his slow descent into her smooth greeting. The second kiss came like thunder from a darkening sky, bringing instant panic, breathlessness, and wonder. She gave herself over to all of it, welcomed every long-dormant sensation. Her synapses crackled with the friction their bodies created. The cry went up inside her head, *Bring on the lightning!* But it came through her weak throat in the form of a lowly whimper.

"Something wrong?"

"No," she gasped. "Not at all." She gripped his shoulders to steady herself. "Just that I was going to show you the ledger drawings, and, unfortunately, they're in my bedroom."

"How is that unfortunate?"

"It's too easy? It looks bad? I don't know." She gave a nervous laugh. "I'm out of my depth, as you can probably tell."

"I don't see anything bad. Do you? Should I scout out the room to see if we're making a bad impression on somebody else?" He questioned three dark doorways with a look and a gesture before she nodded, yes, that was the room. He drew her by the hand, shouting, "Angela, are you in there?"

"That's *hardly* funny."

"What else?" he demanded. "Oh, yeah, too easy. You want to put up an obstacle course?" Approaching the bedroom door, he pushed a ladder-back chair across the wood floor until it blocked their way to the bedroom. "Make me jump through hoops, walk across hot coals. I'm game."

"Oddly enough, I'm an amateur at courting games, Thomas, working off memories that go back to—way too many years to count."

"Then stop counting." He pushed the chair out of the way. "There. Obstacle aside, easy as that. Now bring out the ledger drawings, and let's put this question of age into some perspective."

She turned on the closest lamp—the small one on the vanity—and headed directly for the armoire, where her latest purchases had been secreted.

"Well, I'll be damned," Thomas said behind her back. "What are you doing here, Mom?"

Cassandra spun around to find him grinning over a picture he'd found on her vanity. "Oh, you! That's Aaron's class."

"I'll turn it over." He flashed her a wink. "Just in case you get to suckin' on her baby's face again."

"*Me?* You mean in case her big *baby* . . ." Her prediction dissolved into a giggle and a growl, both from the once sophisticated throat of Cassandra Westbrook. She clicked on the bedside lamp and laid the black leather portfolio open on the bed. "Come over here, baby, and look at my treasures."

"Aw, mama, show me the ones I haven't seen yet."

But he sat on the bed as she spread out the drawings, and they gave each piece due consideration, remarking over the details and putting together the story told by a man who had spent two years in prison for the crime of trying to defend his home and his people from raiders and poachers.

"You're going to display all of them?" Thomas asked.

"I haven't decided. I want to be able to see them every day. On the other hand, I have a request from the university here and another in Chicago. These have virtually been buried for decades."

"Chicago? So you're thinking White Bull might be part of the Bulls family from Chicago." He nodded, totally deadpan. "I'd say the chances are slim to none."

"We're all related," she reminded him.

"All right, mama, you can touché me all to hell, but White Bull's people aren't likely to see his drawings if you put them out on loan in Chicago. And I'd call that a damn shame."

She looked up, her face suddenly warm and stinging. "How about if I publish them in a book? Then they can all have their own copies," she suggested diffidently.

"There's a college on the reservation. It's not as big as the U, but they could provide a good home for these."

Carefully she began replacing the acid-free paper separators between the drawings. "What kind of security could they provide for, say, an exhibition?"

"Not much, but I can check into it." He glanced at her armoire. "What kind of security do you have here?"

"Frankly, I need to upgrade." She held up the last drawing, which was called *Dance at Crow Creek*. It depicted dancers, dwellings, dogs, horses, children, all looking very dignified and orderly. Yet there was a sense of anticipation, as though toes were tapping beneath the blankets and leggings. "Your style is reminiscent of his. Is that a conscious rendering on your part?"

"How could it be?" He lay back on the bed and stared at the ceiling. "You said yourself, these haven't seen the light of day since the recently deceased collector acquired them from the family of the brave army colonel who confiscated them from White Bull."

"I don't think the word *confiscated* was used in the brochure."

He chuckled, a deep rumble in his chest. "The word *gift* sounds so much better. A *gift* to the colonel for his generosity and kindness to the prisoners. Indians are great gift givers."

"I know." She tucked the drawings into their portfolio.

"I wonder how the term *Indian giver* came to mean taking gifts back? They don't do that, do they?"

"They?" He turned to his side and propped himself on his elbow. "What do you see when you look at me?"

"A man," she said.

"I'll take that," he said, leaning across her to shut off the lamp. "It's a start."

"I see an incredibly interesting and attractive man who makes me question my sanity because of the way—" She had to catch her breath when he drew himself back slowly, sliding against her, settling over her in the dim light, taking her in his arms. "—the way I feel when you look at me."

"Tell me about it." His warm breath filled her ear, then swept along the side of her neck, going cool over the wet places he made with his tongue. When she shivered, she felt him smile against her skin. "That's telling."

"Telling what?"

"What moves you."

He drew her slinky skirt up her bare leg as he kissed her down, down, down until she sank into the plush pile of pillows at the head of the bed. His hand inched up, up, up until it cupped her bottom. Now she knew why she had visited the luxury lingerie department after she'd left the hair salon. If she was going to be caught with her skirt up, she wanted to be wearing black silk bikini panties.

She was sure he whispered, "Sweet," but he was nuzzling into the neckline of her sweater, so she wasn't sure what pleased him—the scent of breasts or the feel of silk or the shape of her bottom.

All of the above, she told herself. And everything below, as well.

"Surprised?" she whispered, eliciting an affirmative sound from him. "I expect surprises from you, too."

"The best part is—" He drew himself up and wet his lips, his eyes promising her more wet things. "I can keep them coming all night long."

His kissed her mouth, engaged searching tongue, mouth-to-mouth breath pinching, mouth-to-mouth resuscitation. The luscious feel of mouth on mouth was her first surprise. Mouth kissing through silk, tongue somehow touching private parts by dancing on public parts, teeth sweetly menacing, giving sharp, barely bearable pleasure.

"Oh, my sweet lord, Thomas, I can't. I don't . . ." *Don't want to burst out of my skin, tear off burning clothes, claw at you, bite at you. . . .* "I don't have all night, Thomas."

"Hell, neither do I."

He sat up, chest heaving, pouring a hot stare over her as he unbuckled his belt. "Looking for a quickie? If you're going to change your order, do it now."

"What are we thinking, Thomas?"

"What? Are we *thinking,* Cassandra? That's the problem, then. Thinking does it every—"

"No, please." She sat up quickly, grabbing his hands. "Don't go thinking badly of me."

"Little girl." He chuckled, shaking his head. "I won't be thinking anything of you except that you don't know what you want."

"I do know what I want, and that's the problem." She

drew his arms around her and clutched his broad shoulders. "I want your hands all over me, and I've been telling myself to keep my hands off you. Such a problem, wanting my friend's son."

"I asked you to let that go." He smoothed her hair back from her face and pierced her doubts, eye to eye. "Now I'm going to make you do it, Cassandra. I'm going to take that problem away. I'm comin' on strong. Are you ready for me?"

"What does 'strong' mean?"

"It's a surprise," he muttered against her mouth.

There were many surprises in store, but her own response to his every deft move was the most liberating wonder of wonders. Suddenly nothing mattered but that Thomas wanted Cassandra, only Cassandra, truly and surely Cassandra. Nothing else mattered because Cassandra wanted Thomas, and if she couldn't have him deep dark down inside her, she didn't want to see the sun again.

She told him as much. He made her tell him. He made her call his name out, over and over again, every name she knew for him and a few that flew from her tongue without her knowing and made him laugh, and, oh! the way he moved, the way he touched, the way the vibration from that joyous sound came rumbling into her and made her shoot for the moon.

His shots and shouts echoed hers.

She held on to him, even though he made no move to leave her, and she must have dozed a bit, or passed out, or simply left her quivering body to find some starry place to cache the treasure he'd given her. Her next awareness came deep down, where he grew to fill her, moved to thrill her . . .

"Again?" she whispered.

"Tell me."

"Again, Thomas."

"Tell me more." He drew her legs up high, over his shoulders. "Special orders won't upset me now."

"I can't think of any, except . . ." Oh, his hand. His hand, hand, fingers, thumb . . . "Don't stop."

"The best part," he reminded her in a deep, breathy, haunted, less-than-steady voice, "is that I can . . . keep it coming . . . as long . . . as you want me."

And she wanted him. She left him no doubt.

He took pains not to disentangle himself too much as he tossed a silky fringed throw over their dewy bodies. They got wet together; they would dry together. But there would be no chill. He would have her drifting in dreams of him when he slipped away.

She stirred in his arms. He had to turn to his back to keep himself from rising to meet her every move, but he kept her cuddled against his side. "Did I do you right?" he whispered.

"You did."

"Problem solved, then."

"Sort of. I stopped thinking." She caressed his baby-smooth chest, reminding him that his adolescent chest-hair watch had been in vain. "But I won't stop hoping that your mother and I can still be friends. I'm probably closer to her age than yours."

"Damn," he muttered through the wall of his teeth. "Cassandra, I've been a man for as long as you've been a woman, or damn near. Angela is too young to be my real mother. Birth mother, or whatever you want to call it. When I first met her, she had all kinds of problems, and I helped her out. For one thing, I found her a job."

"You also found her a husband."

"She told you that?" He drew a deep breath. Bad enough she had to bring up his mother at a time like this. "I guess I did. My dog, Jesse."

"Which means he was your friend?"

"He was my hero. He could do anything. The original 'take a bite out of crime' dog. You know that commercial? Jesse could even take the bite out of the dog. He was that cool. Even after we found out he'd been a cop, he was cool. He went back to being a cop, but he was still cool. I trusted him like . . ." He chuckled. "Like my dog. Dark Dog was my first superhero comic book."

"But he's fallen from grace."

"Only mine." The silk blanket slid away from his shoulders as he tucked it carefully around hers. "But we were talking about Angela, who used to be your friend, but now she's your problem. You're afraid she won't approve of you robbing her cradle."

"I wouldn't put it quite that way. I'm not afraid. We're really not that close."

He chuckled as he swung his legs over the side of the bed. "We hardly know each other."

"I meant—"

"I know you don't have all night, and—" With a glance at her watch after brushing his lips across her wrist, he gave out a whistle. "Mama, it's way past this homeboy's bedtime."

66

"All right!" She sat up, and the blanket fell down, exposing her sweet breasts. "Point taken. I'm taking myself too seriously. Or you, maybe. Or this, tonight. That's your point, isn't it?"

He had a point, all right, and her two much prettier ones were pitilessly nagging at it.

"I wasn't trying to make a point. I was just joking with you." He leaned over to kiss her, and damn, if she didn't—right underneath his kiss—scoot over to sit beside him, clutching the fringed throw in her lap.

He topped off the big kiss with a small one. "I still have work to do, and I get my best ideas at night." He gave a nod in the direction of the street in front of her house, where his car was parked, big as life. "And you don't want the neighbors peeking out their windows in the morning and observing my departure."

"Wouldn't that cause a stir?" She giggled girlishly, then grabbed his arm, stroked it a bit, and whispered, "I don't do this, Thomas. I'm not"—her smile nearly undid him—"the merry widow."

"You're not a ho?" His arm served as a crook around her neck, hauling her forehead to his laughing lips for a patently patronizing kiss. "Believe me, Cassandra, nobody's ever going to mistake you for a woman of experience. You ain't no Mrs. Robinson."

"I was a disappointment, then?"

"No." He grinned at her. "*She* was."

It felt good when they laughed together. She looked so sweet with her hair all messed around and her makeup all kissed away.

He adjusted the little blanket across her lap.

"Every time I see you, you're stylin', looking so fine and perfectly put together. You got all the confidence money can buy hanging over your shoulders. You let me take it from you, piece by piece. I could feel you quiver a little bit each time I pushed a piece of your clothing aside. I stripped you of all that stylish security. You know what I found?"

She shook her head.

"The beauty that's all you, only you. No artist could improve on this." He drew his fingers along her jaw, admiring the soft shadows under her eyes, the little lines at their corners. "Some try, but not me. I make a cipher and use it to tell a story. Sometimes I get so wrapped up in the story that I keep to myself for weeks. I forget that paper fantasies are no substitute for the touch of flesh on flesh."

"And you came here for that?"

"I came here hoping. I came wanting and found you feeling the same way." He smiled into her eyes. "Even though we hardly know each other, and you don't have all night."

"The night is slipping away, but I'll gladly give you what's left."

He shook his head. "I really do keep strange studio hours. Late night for mood, into the early morning for virgin sunlight and color. Tonight I have new fantasies to flesh out." He dropped his hand to her shoulder, caressed her collarbone with his thumb. "Or maybe old fantasies to flesh out in new ways."

"May I see your studio sometime?"

"It's also where I live."

She pleaded with a smile. "Then I guess I'm angling for an invitation to your bachelor pad as well."

"It's nothing like this. Aaron and I decided we'd have our first workday here. Get him out of school and me out of the garret for the day. Is that okay?"

"I can either be here or not, whichever the two of you prefer. I go to the gallery almost every day, but, of course, I'm flexible."

"I noticed. Do you work out?"

"When I have—" A little slow on the uptake, she laughed with him. "Oh, yes. Wasn't that original."

"I want you to be here when it's time for Aaron to go. And then I want you to let me stay awhile." He reached for his pants on the floor. "I want to see your whole collection."

"Piece by piece," she agreed, handing him the shirt she had unbuttoned earlier. "One per visit."

"I like that plan."

He left by the back door, even though his car was parked at the front curb. The back door was sheltered by shrubbery and a vine-covered arbor. It made the house vulnerable, he thought, but it also provided secrecy for a lover's exit.

Was that who he was? A lover?

Tonight he had become Cassandra's lover. He wondered if taking a lover was something most wealthy young widows did eventually. Clearly there was no reason for them to get married when they had everything they needed except a man.

And now Cassandra *had* a man. She wouldn't be hanging on some old rich fart's arm. She had

Thomas Warrior.

He passed his car and crossed the street, hopped over a stone retaining wall, and made his way among the carefully pruned trees lining one of the city's loveliest lakes. A huge old maple offered a sheltered place to linger for a moment, look across the lake, and think about being a lady's lover. He'd told Angela time and time again that he wasn't interested in girls. Ah, but this woman of his—*his* woman?—his woman had a girlish side to her. He liked that about her. He liked everything about her.

He'd been lonely. He couldn't admit that to himself until now, but it was true. Thomas didn't enjoy being a loner. He'd tried so hard to keep his family together when he was a kid, but his father had disappeared, and his mother had been a ghost in his barren world even before she'd given up the ghost in a roadside ditch. All he'd had left was his brother.

But he'd managed to put together a second family. With Angela and Jesse, he'd become part of the Brown Wolf clan, and he hadn't given them up entirely. He knew what family meant, even if Jesse did not. First and foremost, it meant loyalty. Tommy T Little Warrior was nothing if not fiercely loyal.

His breath made puffs of mist as he smiled against the darkness, remembering the way Cassandra had called his name—Thomas, Warrior, Tom, Tommy, Tommy T. In answer to her call, he'd crowded all of them into her big, beautiful bed.

What a view she had, he thought as he gazed across the lake. Lights twinkling in the water, the mist that would rise in the morning as those lights blinked out, the autumn colors that would come to life in the sunlight, and the joggers, the women pushing babies in strollers, the kids on their in-line skates each day.

Did she wave to them when she came outside in the morning to collect her newspaper? Did she know her neighbors? Did she attend a Christmas party every year at the house next door?

For his own part, he would have to answer no. He had come a long way from the kid living in the streets, but to him the city was sometimes still a lonely place.

A single maple leaf drifted in front of him, changing direction all on its own in the still of the night, landing silently in the grass.

chapter 6

JESSE BROWN WOLF LOVED BEING A COP, but there were times when he hated thinking like one.

Anybody could break the law, and it was probably safe to say that everybody did. So many laws, so many choices. A cop's world was black and white. No gray. Gray could throw a cop's head into a deep hole. If a guy wanted to keep his head on straight, he put his actions into one of two columns: a black one titled Wrong, and a white one called Right. The first column was a list of everything a person could do that was illegal. The second column simply said "Not doing anything listed in the other column."

Jesse had been there. He had lost touch with the rules of common sense and shaken off the reins of humility because a supercop could do no wrong. It had cost his young son his life and thrown Jesse's miserable head into a pit of pain. Then Angela and Tommy T had come along, pulled him out of the pit, and made him strong enough to deal with the pain.

He was strong enough to step into the black-and-white traces again and think like a cop. For Jesse, it was either do the job right or not at all. But in doing it right, he had lost another son. He couldn't expect Tom to forget that Jesse had taken part in his brother's arrest, testified at his trial, and helped to put him away for seven years. But he had hoped to be forgiven. Tom was a good man, a gifted man. He should have grown to realize that Stony had left Jesse no choice. He had been through treatment, rehab, counseling—every program Jesse could find for him, but he couldn't stay clean. He was hell-bent on destroying himself and taking a bunch of ragtag street kids with him.

Jesse had done what he'd had to do. For now, reading Thomas Warrior's comic books was as close as he could get to his adopted son.

Comic book? He turned the book over and checked the back cover just to make sure he'd read the receipt correctly. He'd paid eighteen bucks for this baby. They called this one a graphic novel and priced it accordingly.

He was just setting the book aside on his desk in favor of finishing his paperwork and getting his butt home in time for supper for a change when Officer Garrett Murphy, one of Tom's most avid fans, popped in for his usual poorly timed bull session. Murphy never worried about paperwork. If there was a God, one of these days it would catch up to him.

"What's up, my man?" Murphy snatched up the book. "Hey, is this a new one?"

"Get your own copy." Jesse gestured for the return of his property. "I just picked that one up at the bookstore. How do they expect kids to come up with the price of a comic book these days? It's outrageous."

"The least he could do is hook his ol' man up with a free book." Murphy settled a butt cheek on the corner of Jesse's desk and started flipping through the book.

"I can buy my own copy, but I can't see too many twelve-year-olds paying this much." Jesse punched Murphy's thigh. "Get off my reports, man. That's two hours worth of—"

"These aren't for twelve-year-olds," Murphy observed, pausing in his page-thumbing for a closer look. "Man, that Victory is some hot babe. Tom does some nice work. He writes the story, too, right? He's not just doing the artwork."

"He does it all," Jesse said, turning his attention back to the notes he'd made during his last shift.

"What do they say on TV? 'Ripped from the head-lines.'" Murphy slapped the open book with the back of his hand. "Man, Tom is right on top of today's news with this story."

Jesse looked up from his notebook. "What, the Vic-tor/Victory thing? He's not a cross-dresser or anything like that. It's kind of a mystical transformation."

"I'm talking about the theft of Native American art.

We've got an investigation going on right now. I'm surprised they haven't tapped you for some of your contacts."

"Tom is the only Indian artist I know. Are they stealing his stuff?"

"It's more like antique stuff. Artifacts. Like this." Murphy flipped the book around and pointed to a series of pictures showing Victor removing a ghost shirt and a buffalo robe from a mannequin in some kind of display. "What's that saying about life imitating art?"

"I think you've got it backward."

"No, I know what I'm talkin' about, man. It's a saying."

"You're saying Tom is giving somebody ideas? If he can switch them from wearing long black coats and taking assault rifles to school to stealing antiques, I'm all for it." Jesse took the book from Murphy's hand and set it out of his reach. "This just came out. It's probably been in the works for months."

"No doubt, but I gotta show you something."

Murphy disappeared from the doorway, returning momentarily with the Metro section of the *Star Tribune*, which he tossed, folded to reveal the picture of a painted buffalo robe and the clever headline "Only the Buffalo Roams."

"Coincidence? Or some mystical connection between art and life? You decide, Dog."

Murphy enjoyed dropping the cool quote, leaving Jesse to wonder where he'd heard it before. Did he care? Not much, but he did care about the fact that the man wouldn't quit calling him Dog.

. . .

CASSANDRA SLEPT LATER THAN USUAL, woke up feeling better than usual, and lingered longer than usual in her canopied bed, enjoying the new scent on her soft sheets. Thomas Warrior was the first man she had shared the bed and the sheets with, even for a few hours. It was the bed's first time.

The décor in her bedroom was all female, all Cassandra. She had enjoyed having her own bedroom for several years before Edgar's death. She'd felt a little guilty about wanting it, but enjoyed having it, loved decorating it according to her own taste, cherished her privacy.

But, ah, the scent that surrounded her was spicy, sexy, thoroughly intoxicating. She might decide to lie in bed all day, swaddled in her elegant cotton sheets, wallowing in sensual remembrances of the night before. She had it coming, after all. Her sister, for one, would say so. Cassie was due some of this feel-good time.

Darcy? She was looking for Darcy's approval now? Bad sign, she told herself as she flipped the tempting sheets away from her naked body. The morning chill was bracing. Good for the skin, good for the soul.

Wake up, Cassie. Smell the coffee. The difference between thirty and forty is a lifetime. The next time you see Thomas Warrior, he'll be with his girlfriend.

In her mind, Cassandra had already started rounding her age off to forty. She'd added a year to her age when she'd started seeing Edgar, and she'd kept it ever since. It was her ace-in-the-hole year. She could be as old and sophisticated as she wanted to be.

She did feel a little strange standing in her closet stark naked, searching for something to wear. Bathing was the sum total of what she did in the nude. She loved clothes.

Smooth pleated slacks and designer shirts with French cuffs—that was Cassandra's idea of casual. She had a pair of jeans in there somewhere, but she never wore them. She loved the power of the jacketed sheath or the well-cut suit. Stripped of her chic wardrobe, her upscale address, her unique art collection and her swanky gallery, who would she be?

The beauty contestant from Frogtown.

She and Darcy had been taught to trade on their looks. It was the only kind of game plan their mother could seem to come up with.

So you want to go to college, Cassie? Where are we going to get the money? They give you a scholarship if you win this contest. Lose some weight and put on some makeup.

Darcy, honey, you're just not college material. You need a man. Preferably a rich man. Cozy up to the right man, and you've got it made.

Darcy tried, but she kept making it with the wrong man. She and Aaron were the only family Cassandra had, so there was no question about helping as much as she could. But helping Darcy was never a simple bailout. There were always complications—always an imminent deadline, a blade ready to drop, some wolf crouching in the bushes or—the worst complication of all—a bottom line that required her to choose between her principles and her sister. She had even asked Darcy to stop telling her what the money was for, forego the detail about what she'd gotten herself into this time. Cassandra didn't want to know.

But Darcy always had to tell her. It was part of the ritual.

Cassandra had run into Darcy's latest boyfriend once, which was once too often. His idea of sweet talk was "Hey, sugar, how about getting off your fat ass and getting the damn phone?" She'd tried to question Darcy's sanity with a furtive what-are-you-doing-with-this-creep look, but Darcy wouldn't make eye contact with her. When the "fat ass" epithet had also been applied to Aaron, Cassandra had, in a few well-chosen words, spoken her mind on her way out the door as she'd taken Aaron to a movie.

It had taken Darcy another month to show the boyfriend the same door.

Which had clearly not been soon enough.

THOMAS'S CREATIVE JUICES WERE FLOWING. He didn't know what had inspired him more—revisiting the ledger drawings in Cassandra's bedroom or visiting Cassandra's bed. Both were magical.

Cassandra reminded him of Victory. They both used beauty and class to protect themselves from mere mortal men. Because they didn't completely trust their femininity, they persisted in shielding their womanhood.

The comparison was intriguing, but Thomas couldn't take it too far. Victory never compromised, and so remained apart. Cassandra was as mortal as he was. Her ultimate shyness was titillating. It had been lovely to watch the woman reclaim the powers of the wildness and wonder she must have enjoyed once, before she'd tamped them down.

Thomas smiled at Victory. "Who would you choose for a mate? What kind of superman could ring Victory's chimes? Toll her bells?"

The answer came to him in a vision of ledger pages lifted by the wind from a blanket and blown one by one across the decades. They flew in close formation, each one arched like a white sail wending its way in the blue.

A hunter riding a horse fast enough to run down an antelope.

The same magnificent horse ground-tied behind a clump of wild plum bushes, heavy with fruit, waiting for the hunter to pick his target from a pretty flock of wild turkeys along a riverbank.

Hunter becomes dancer, dressed in finery and feathers and surrounded by his fellow hunters with a nice lineup of well-dressed women doing their own thing on the side.

Hunter becomes warrior, putting himself and his horse between the people of the past and the enemy that was the future.

This is who I am, the man in the drawings told Victory. *Will you not embrace me?*

Thomas could barely shape one sketch before another came to him. His hand translated the vision from the past into figures and faces that would function in his own world, which was part twenty-first-century Midwestern city and part timeless earthy fantasy. But his images were infused with the straightforward honesty of the ledger art, new colors and clarity and simple beauty. The work left Thomas feeling spent and dizzy, as though he'd been caught up in a whirlwind. A few early hours had seemed like a full day. For the first time in months, maybe years, he slept deeply, hard, totally fulfilled.

elsewhere

VICTOR FOUND HIS MARCHING ORDERS ON the drafting table. They were splendid. Thomas Warrior's creative talent was godlike. Victor recognized the inestimable value of ledger drawings immediately and accepted his weighty charge eagerly. His final mission could come at any time. If this turned out to be his swan song, so be it. Thomas had chosen a treasure worth dying for.

And the way he was laying the groundwork with the "owner" was totally brilliant—getting his man into the house and getting his rocks off all in one fell swoop. Thomas obviously had talent he hadn't even begun to tap into.

In the guise of a lunch-hour jogger, Victor scouted the neighborhood by day to get his bearings. He was as familiar with the two cities that faced off over the Mississippi as he was with the intricacies of his favorite tattoo, but the houses on the lakes were a world away from his stomping grounds. They were lousy with security systems. Most of the owners put up signs declaring exactly what kind of system they had, which was help-ful.

By night, he had a closer look at the house and the woman. The absence of any barking was a promising sign. He walked into the yard carrying a stray cat he'd befriended with a few morsels of food. If anyone spotted him, he was out chasing down his girlfriend's cat.

He wasn't impressed with the security system, but the woman was classy, even in her nightclothes. Plenty of low windows on the ground floor gave him a good view as she took a phone call, gathered some magazines, turned off a lamp, helped herself to a glass of red wine. He'd heard her voice on the phone, but this was his first glimpse of her. She looked very much the way he'd pic-tured her in his mind. Untouchable.

But Thomas had made his way past that look, and for Victor, the thought of touching the untouchable was almost stimulating. Not that he could or would, but now that he had seen her, he could think about it. Something different, something new.

"Something dangerous."

Victor dropped the cat at the sound of Victory's voice.

"Are you going to risk compromising our mission by becoming a Peeping Tom?"

"Peeping *Tom?*" Victor nearly choked on a stifled laugh. "Thomas would howl if he heard that."

"He would do more than howl if he saw what I'm looking at, which is a fool."

"It's in my nature. You know the Trickster's nature."

"You are the bane of my existence, Victor."

"Ah, but I'm necessary."

"Yes, you are. But your lustful thoughts are not. Banish them from your mind and do what you came to do. How will you liberate the old drawings from this house?"

"I'm here to determine the best way."

"That's right. You're here to find the key. That woman is not the key. You will leave her to Thomas."

"I will," he promised as he took to the trees.

But he couldn't promise to leave all thoughts of her to Thomas.

chapter 7

TOM PICKED AARON UP AT SCHOOL AND headed for Cassandra's house. Aaron was upbeat, eager to begin his new program. Tom was equally upbeat, eager for the moment when Cassandra would greet them at the door. It had been three days. They had been productive days, but he'd been surprisingly impatient for their passing. His productivity was generally all that really mattered to him, but this week, Friday mattered. Seeing Cassandra again mattered more than he would have predicted three days ago.

"All the kids at school are dying to know who my mentor is," Aaron told him as they drove around the lake. "Especially after Mrs. Brown Wolf told them that your artwork had made it into books and stuff."

"You haven't told them, have you?"

"No, but I wish I could. They'd be so jealous." Aaron

looked like a different kid when he smiled. It was the first time Tom had seen anything resembling youthful light in the boy's eyes. He was pale, overweight, under-styled in the hair department, and dressed for school, not for cool.

Tom returned the smile as he parked his car in front of the house. "They're jealous anyway. You're getting out of school."

"I don't mind being in school. I just don't like it when they bother me when I'm trying to draw." He clutched a large, dog-eared accordion file in his pudgy hands. "It's gonna be hard keeping my promise to only draw on Fridays. Except, you know, if it's part of something else we're doing, like social studies."

"Yeah, well, that's the deal, man. You keep your promise, and I'll keep mine." Aaron was dragging something out of the neck of his sweater as they headed up the sidewalk. "What's that?"

"My keys." He slipped the long chain over his head and dangled two keys for Tom to examine. "Aunt Cassie gave me a key to the back door. She said she fixed up a studio for us. A *real* studio."

"That was nice of her. How 'bout we ring the bell and let her know she has company?"

"She's probably gone already." Aaron took the fork in the sidewalk, galumphing like a baby rhino. "She said she might be back at lunchtime," he called out over his shoulder.

Disappointed, Tom followed the boy through the back door and into the quiet house.

Aaron led the way through the living room and down

a long hall. "It's the little den in back—that's our studio."

"I thought she'd showed me all the rooms where she keeps her Native American art." Tom stood in the doorway, impressed with the lighting she'd provided, the oak library table with adjustable desk chairs placed at either end. She'd clearly cleaned out some art supply store and stocked the shelves with pencils, paint, and paper sufficient to equip the Disney studios.

But it was the display of Native artwork and artifacts that interested Tom the most, especially the fringed, painted deerskin shirt that hung on the wall.

"She doesn't use this room much since Uncle Edgar died," Aaron said. "I think he slept in here a lot when he couldn't go up and down the stairs by himself anymore."

"He must have been pretty sick."

"Yeah, but he was old, too. And crabby. But if you said anything to Aunt Cassie about it, she would say, 'He wasn't always like this.'" He set his portfolio on the huge table. "I get to come over more now that he's dead. He didn't like kids."

"So, you don't miss old Uncle Edgar."

"Nope. Besides, he was really bad off. A lot of people came to his funeral, though. He wasn't as famous as you, but my mom said a lot of people worked for him." Aaron's face brightened. "I'll bet when you die, it'll be all over the news."

Tom laughed. "If I wanted to be in the news, I wouldn't have to die to make it happen."

"I would." The light vanished from the boy's eyes, leaving Tom to wonder whether he'd imagined it. "It would have to be something really bad, like a serial killer or a plane crash."

"Making the news is highly overrated," Tom said as he claimed a chair and rolled it across the wood floor toward its twin. "Whether it's for doing or dying, you know what I'm saying? Live your life, Aaron. Don't worry about playing it out for somebody else." He nodded toward chairs, almost said, *Take a load off,* but caught himself in time. "Have a seat."

They sat kitty-corner from each other, Aaron lovingly pulling a sheaf of papers from his portfolio, Tom wondering what the hell he was doing sitting knee to knee with any kind of onlooker—never mind a kid perfectly suited to the Addams family—thinking he was going to do any drawing. He absolutely never let anyone watch him. . . .

Good God. Tom had seen some dark drawings, but the faces and the places coming out of Aaron's portfolio were as grim as it got. Worse, they were well executed and grim. How old was this kid? Twelve? Thirteen? Where had he seen stuff like this? Tom held fast to his expressionless demeanor as he took in the high level of skill and the murky mood each drawing revealed. The anatomy of a woman wearing some sort of claw necklace, blood streaming over bare breasts, was amazingly accurate. And chilling.

"These are your favorites, huh? The good stuff?"

"Yeah," Aaron enthused. He pulled a portrait—literally a handsome devil—from the pile. "This is Silver Claw. He's like a vampire, but he doesn't turn into a bat. He turns into a woman, sort of like Victor does."

"Victor doesn't turn into a woman, exactly. He's the

part of Victory that can't transcend mortality."

"Yeah, well, he's *not* Victor. I didn't copy you. This guy's way more powerful than Victor. And he doesn't only need blood to survive. Look." Another apt rendering of a wretched soul emerged from the portfolio. "He consumes the heart before it stops beating."

"No way," Tom whispered, trying to balance genuine admiration against equally genuine concern for the kid's mental state.

"It's possible. I checked it out on the Internet. I always research everything to make sure it's true to a certain point. You know what I mean?"

Tom nodded, still trying to imagine Aaron coming up with the details of Silver Claw's repast. "You use the Internet a lot?"

"There's some cool stuff on the Internet. Pictures that show everything, people who can answer any question you can think of. You can go to a chat room and find out all kinds of stuff."

"That can be useful, but I hear it can be a little dicey." Tom had done the chat room thing and ultimately found it boring. "Depends on who you're talking to and what you're looking for."

"You don't always know who you're talking to," Aaron said.

"You got that right. Who told you about the beating heart thing?"

"I got that from a couple of different sites—one on open heart surgery, one about cannibalism, and—"

"Shut up, man! Cannibalism?"

"It had pictures."

"Aaron, my man, we are gonna start this mentorship with some basic guidelines about how we gotta work it." Tom laid a hand on the boy's shoulder. "First, we need to trust each other. Like you're showing me your special drawings here, and I gotta tell you, you've got talent. But I'm gonna trust you with a little secret. My stuff isn't this gory. You know why?"

"Doesn't it sell?"

"Oh, it sells, but only in certain places. There's a more basic reason. And this is the secret." Tom gave a sheepish smile. "I've got a weak stomach."

"Now *you* shut up."

"I ain't lyin'. So the first time you come up with something that makes me puke, it's all over."

"All over Aunt Cassie's Persian rug," Aaron said with a laugh. He was one up on his mentor.

"All over, period. No cannibalism. Okay?"

"How about rats? Eating rats?"

"Now, that's different. You can definitely do rats. But you've gotta cook 'em. We're civilized storytellers, you and me."

"Yeah, okay." Aaron carefully placed the drawing of Silver Claw at dinner back in the folder. "Aunt Cassie says you're a Sioux Indian."

"Speaking of civilized," Tom chimed in with a smile.

"How come you don't look like an Indian?"

"Do I look like a black man?"

"Kind of, but . . ."

"My dad was African-American. Mrs. Brown Wolf is my adopted mother, but my real mother was mostly Lakota, which is Sioux Indian. They were both a little bit white. You mix them all together, and what you see is what you get."

"Can you speak your Indian language?"

Tom shook his head. "Wish I could."

"You don't talk like the black kids at school, either."

"I'm not a kid. I see you don't make all your characters look alike, which is good. Not all vampires look like Dracula."

"They're not really vampires. Their teeth are more like a cat's, and they have retractable claws."

Tom rolled his chair over to the supply shelf. "I guess your mom doesn't limit your web access with any filters?"

"She wouldn't know how. I got my computer from Aunt Cassie. Mom doesn't get into it much."

"They have undercover cops working those chat rooms now," Tom said as he sorted through pencils, selecting an array of numbers. "You start asking too many questions about how to prepare fillet of human, somebody might come looking for you."

"I'll tell him I'm a civilized storyteller. Like Thomas Warrior."

"Don't go gettin' my name mixed up in no cannibal's cook pot, man. I don't want cops *or* cannibals comin' around my door."

He tossed several sheets of drawing paper over to the table and grabbed a gum eraser as he pushed off the cabinet and rolled himself back to the table. He overshot and had to walk his wheels back to the table.

"You're not making marks on the floor, are you?"

Tom peered over his shoulder. "I don't know. Am I?"

87

"Uncle Edgar would have a piss fit."

"Dead men don't piss," Tom quipped. He slid Aaron a wink as he picked out a fight sketch he thought had potential. "Let's take this panel and play with viewpoint. You know what I mean by that? Viewpoint?"

Aaron immersed himself in his drawing session, but Tom's attention was divided between engaging himself in Aaron's work and listening for sounds of Cassandra. He didn't intend to leave without seeing her. But he let Aaron be the one to say "Aunt Cassie must be home." He got a kick out of hearing the boy call her Aunt Cassie.

Tom nodded. "Finish up what you've got going there."

"You guys must have put in a long time," she said when she appeared in the doorway. "School's been out for a couple of hours."

"I guess I didn't hear the bell." Tom turned, savoring the jump-start the sight of her gave his internal engine. But he wasn't about to let it show, except to look her in the eye and say, "Hello."

"Hi." Too soft to last, her smile was overtaken by immediate business. "Aaron, your mom will be here in a few minutes. I just spoke with her. It must have gone well, then."

"*Ex*cellent," Aaron drawled. He showed off the four-paneled action sequence he'd just finished.

"Excellent," said his aunt.

"Excellent," his mentor agreed. "I'm glad you hooked us up. We'll get the mess cleaned up."

"I don't see a mess. I don't even see any evidence of a refrigerator or pantry raid."

"We weren't doing raids today," Tom said. "My man here is honing his perspective, getting in touch with his sensitive side. I'll coach him in the fine art of pantry raiding some other time."

"If you're hungry—" A car horn interrupted Cassandra's offer.

"It's Mom!" Aaron grabbed his latest drawings and made for the door. "She'll like these."

"How about a thank-you?" Cassandra said.

"Don't forget your portfolio," Tom added.

Aaron complied with both reminders and hurried out the door, leaving silence after the distant slam.

Tom waited for her to speak or move or even breathe, but as far as he could tell, she had no breath in her. He was sure she wasn't looking at him. He would have felt it if she were.

"I thought you'd be here today," he said finally.

It took her a moment to answer.

"I thought I'd hear from you after the other night."

"You couldn't hear me thinking about you?" He smiled when she questioned him with a look. "Calling to you in my sleep?"

"I see." She raised her elegant eyebrows. "Keep it light. I'm sorry. I'm not familiar with the protocol for whatever the other night was or might become."

"Uh-oh." He glanced at her feet. "I didn't see you standing on the protocol. Did I step on some toes?"

"I'm not sure where I stand at all."

Her suddenly tentative tone surprised him. Her crystalline elegance fell away with her admission, leaving her starkly vulnerable.

He took her in his arms for her protection. "We got something going the other night. How do you feel about it becoming more of the same?" He slid his nose into her hair and filled his head with her pastel scent. "Just between us."

"A thing?"

"A thang," he drawled. "Our own thing with its own protocol."

Keeping it light seemed to be working. He could feel the tension draining away, her body giving it all over to his. He rubbed her fine, long back, pressed his fingers along her spine the way his massage therapist did for him after he'd been sitting at his drafting table for too many hours on end—his bottom end.

"How would that work, exactly?" she whispered, tentative but hopeful.

"Can't say, exactly. I liked the way it worked the first time, with the broad strokes and bright colors. I could start adding in the detail if you'll let me stay awhile."

"Isn't that where the devil is?"

"Could be." Seeking the soft down he'd discovered on the side of her neck, he pushed her hair behind her ear. "Or he could be hiding in the protocol."

"Or the pantry," she said, quivering at the touch of his lips to her neck.

"Then it's time I went raiding."

He made love to her on the sofa in the den turned art studio. He took her clothes off, piece by piece, kissing her as he exposed her, stoking his fire with friction from her undulating body.

There was something about her pantyhose that embarrassed her, brought her back to the reality he had driven away. She wanted to take them off herself, but he laughed, stayed her hands with one of his, and used the other to play with her. He teased her about finding the "pantry hose" and assured her that raiders enjoyed the spandex resistance. He loved her legs, and he took special pleasure in liberating them, tossing the pantyhose up and watching them spread their legs and drift to the floor. "Hose, you down," he said with a laugh.

Cassandra tore into his jeans. "I'll show you a hose-down, Thomas Warrior."

"No way, baby, it's definitely up."

"I want it down here," she whispered as she pushed his jeans over his hips. She gave him no chance to take them off, for she took him in her hand and made him forget what he was wearing, where he was, who he was, everything but what he was about, which was sliding into her.

"Way down, Thomas," she whispered in his ear, and he was glad to be Thomas instead of Tom or Tommy or Tommy T, because that hot *S* made him shiver in a good way.

"Way down, Thomas . . . way-y-y oooh, Thooo-maaaas . . ."

"Yo, Cassandra," he whispered. "Hosin' you down, honey."

And she met him, matched him, pitched him up and flew with him, reaching heights neither of them had ever imagined.

For unmeasured moments, neither of them wanted to move. Had they been in a bed, he would have slept, possibly through the night. He might have done the thing he had managed to avoid his whole adult life—ruin a silky night with a sandpaper morning.

Fortunately, the sofa put a cramp in his sleeping style. But he wasn't ready to leave her. The night was feeling so smooth and sweet, and the wine she brought him added mellow to the list. He threw pillows on the floor, made a fire in the fireplace, and curled his nude body around his woman. She had draped a fringed blanket around her shoulders, and she sat on the floor like a serene yogi, sipping her wine and contemplating the fire.

"We didn't quite make it to the bedroom, did we?" she mused as she gave him a sweet-wine, sex-mellow smile.

"I can see us making it in every room in the house. How many are there?" He glanced past her and noticed the full moon rising above the treetops. "We could follow that big, fat moon from window to window."

"It's a big house. Lots of big windows. The bedroom would feel more private."

"The night brings me all the privacy I need. At home I keep my curtains closed during the day, but at night I like them open."

"What's your place like?"

"It's high, and it feels open. It reminds me of a tree house I built with . . ." Clearly he was getting too comfortable, going places he hadn't been in a long time. "With Jesse."

She touched the tattoo on his arm—an exuberant tribute to Dark Dog that he'd designed and had applied after he'd made his first sale. He cringed mentally, anticipating a comment about his artwork or her distaste for tattoos.

But she said, "He seems like a good man."

"He is, mostly. His problem is he can't be wrong, you know what I'm saying? He catches a person in a jam once—okay, more than once, but some people are just unlucky that way—but Jesse gets on his case and there's no letting up. Jesse is all about the letter of the law."

"You had to toe the line," she surmised.

"It was never about me. He set my brother up, and then he busted him. I can't look Jesse in the face without remembering that look in Stony's eyes. You know, like *'Et tu, Brute?'* " He gave a sardonic chuckle and shook his head. "If he heard me say that, he'd damn near die laughing. Schoolboy, he'd call me."

"Stony's your older brother?"

He nodded. "Before I met Angela, it was just Stony and me most of the time. He looked after me the best he could, kept me in school. But after I went to live with her, and then she married Jesse, Stony didn't think there was much room for him."

"Was he guilty?"

"He had no chance to prove otherwise. Sure, he was using again, and, yeah, he was strung out, but he wasn't the one they wanted. They got the guy he was working for to cop a plea and give them a few names up and down the line. It looked good, hauling in a dozen hoods at once. For a big bust like that, who can blame Jesse for giving up Stony Little Warrior?"

"His brother?"

"It's my business to sort out the good guys from the bad guys as much as it is Jesse's," he observed, as though he were finding bits of truth in the fire. "I know where I'm supposed to put Stony and where Jesse fits in. But we grew up in a world where it isn't that easy. All three of us did. When we slept outside, it wasn't in no tree house."

"I didn't grow up in a house like this either."

He welcomed the shift in focus with a smile. "Cassandra and Darcy and who else?"

"Our mother. I don't remember my father very well. He was 'away on business' most of the time. He would bring presents when he came home and make a fuss over Darcy and me, but somewhere along the way he had lost interest in my mother. I was about twelve the last time I saw him. He just went away and never came back." Her shrug unsettled her shawl, exposing her pretty shoulder. "I was determined to go to school, have a career, be independent, but when I met Edgar Westbrook, I got sidetracked."

"The *late* Edgar Westbrook," he amended. "Your ol' man."

"He wasn't old when I married him."

"I meant *your husband.*"

"Old enough to be my father, but I was only . . ." She caught herself, looked at him as though someone in the room had made a gaff. "I can't believe I said that. I've never actually said that."

"Said what?"

"That he was old enough to be my father."

"So what? You're not disrespecting him when you say that. Did you have a good marriage?"

"I think so. Yes, it was fine. I left home and never looked back. But I should have stayed closer to Darcy."

94

She slid down closer to him. "I guess that's why I've been trying to help out with Aaron."

"A computer is a nice gift. He says his mom isn't into computers, so I guess you provided him with Internet access."

"What fun would a computer be without Internet access?"

"I have it myself, but I'm not a big user." He put his arm around her shoulders. "And I'm not a big fan of censorship, but Aaron is pretty young to be cruisin' the information superhighway without any limits, you know what I'm saying?"

"I told Darcy about the parental control feature."

He gave her a think-again look.

"He's looking at pictures he shouldn't be?"

The tilt of his head acknowledged the possibility. Narking the kid over didn't set well with him.

"Nudity?" she persisted.

"Nudity isn't such a bad thing," he said with a sly smile. "Listen, if he thinks I couldn't wait to tell on him, the party's over. He's talented. He's curious. He's resourceful." He paused to choose his words. "And he's got a serious dark side."

"Aaron?"

"I don't claim to be an expert on kids," he hedged. "Maybe it's no big deal, but Angela said he was a quiet kid, a loner."

"But he's a good kid."

"No doubt. But I know my own head was like a sponge at that age. I'd soak up everything around me and squeeze it into my own little creative laboratory. Aaron's head is a lot like mine; it's a sketchpad." He fortified himself with a sip of wine. "That age, it's a touchy time for a kid."

"You still haven't told me what you mean by 'dark side.'"

Tom sighed, still unsure of how much to disclose. Telling went against his grain. He came from the you-want-to-know-so-bad-find-out-yourself school of thought.

But Cassandra was like Angela. *Look at me, talk to me, tell me.*

"Okay, so Aaron has his public portfolio, and he has his personal stash, the drawings he doesn't show anyone, the ones he really cares about. And that's cool." He looked her in the eye on a note of encouragement. "We all do that. Even you."

"I can't draw."

"It's something else, then, but maybe you hardly think about it anymore. With Aaron, it's pretty intense. You need to be real careful about picking out a mentor for a kid like that."

"I was. Angela assured me that if anyone could get him to come out of his shell, it would be you."

"With the kind of stuff he's researching on the Internet, he could run into people who can lure him out of the shell and into some very deep shit." He glanced at the ceiling. "Has he seen the White Bull drawings?"

"No, he hasn't."

"Is it all right if I show them to him, use them for instruction?"

"Of course."

"They're still in the bedroom?"

"I keep meaning to put them downstairs. Should I tell Darcy about this Internet thing?"

He shrugged. "Work with her on the parental control tools first. He's a pretty shy kid. He says he doesn't have any friends. He needs me to be a friend more than anything else right now."

"It's hard to know who to trust these days."

"You got that right." He kissed the lovely shoulder she'd bared for him. "I gotta say, I admire you for taking a real personal interest in checking your nephew's new mentor out thoroughly."

"I gotta say," she echoed as she buried her fingertips in his curly hair, "It's been my pleasure."

"Mine, too."

chapter 8

FOR THE FIRST TIME IN HIS LIFE, THOMAS was discovering that finding pleasure in one woman's company could turn a perfectly good way of life upside down. A happy hermit could suddenly start stepping "out there" at the behest of the right woman. If it could happen to Thomas Warrior, it could happen to anyone.

Lately he'd started wandering away from his desk when he should have been working. He'd called Angela a couple of times, just to see how things were going at home. She went down the list of things that were going, but he could hear a certain expectation in her voice. She knew something was up. Sooner or later, she would ask. Sooner or later, he would tell her, depending on when he had it figured out for himself—sooner, or later.

All he knew now was that his desire to be with Cassandra had to be tempered. He had to walk and talk off the unfamiliar restlessness that plagued him. On more than one occasion, he'd found his way downstairs and served as a teacher's aide during story time.

Story time, for God's sake. But he had to do something. The way he'd been thinking about her, it would be too easy to end up on Cassandra's doorstep looking like a puppy that had fallen off the pound truck. Not cool. Rather than call her and ask to see her on an off day, he was making up stories for the kids downstairs.

It had been years since Tom had permitted himself to become personally involved in real people's lives. He'd had enough of that as a kid. People were a lot of work, and half the time the work was wasted. There was more satisfaction to be had in making the whole thing up—people, places, disasters, solutions—than in hooking up with family and friends on a regular basis. But now that he'd opened the door, he couldn't seem to close it as long as there was a kid standing there with a drawing in his hand.

After a couple of weekly sessions with Aaron, Tom had actually proposed a visit to the science museum and suggested that they take Cassandra and Tom's brother Sam. Tom figured he'd kill two birds with one stone by taking Sam along. He'd been promising to "do something" with his little brother for months. Angela was not above reminding him that he was Sam's personal superhero, and that he ought to make more frequent efforts to live up to his place on the pedestal. He thought his invitation for a day of educational socializing had to look pretty damned heroic, even though he expected to benefit personally from bringing an extra companion along for the lady's nephew.

But Tom's ego was in for a couple of bruises. Cassandra begged off, and Sam had to be bribed. He liked the science museum, but he didn't want to be seen hanging out with Aaron Farmer. "Too geeky," Sam said. The thought that maybe Cassandra had similar concerns about Thomas only proved his theory about relationships with real people. Too damn much work.

Tom put his charm to the test by trying to sell the Vikings display. He wondered aloud how many Minnesotans followed the arrows thinking they were going to see football memorabilia. Sam didn't care about football or Norsemen; he couldn't wait to get to the museum's Omni Theater for a surround-screen shark experience. Aaron was cool with anything Tom suggested—dragon ships, sharks, purple snow cones. In the end it was Tom's little brother who made all the choices.

Tom sat between the boys in the theater. He wanted to "be there" for both of them if they got scared, but the ominous fins, bulbous eyes, and countless pointy teeth flashing above, below, and all around them didn't seem to faze anyone but Tom. It was the motion that hit him hardest. He had forgotten about his one and only boating experience during a squall on Lake Superior, when he'd promised his ancestors from both sides of the world that he would follow their examples from that day forward.

Thomas Warrior was no Viking. His stomach was bred for dry land.

And he was counting the minutes until he could get back to it.

"Aunt Cassie thinks somebody tried to get into her house," Aaron whispered out of the watery blue. "A burglar or something."

Tom listed toward Aaron's side. "Was something stolen?"

"I don't know. We didn't leave the door unlocked the last time, did we?"

"You're responsible for security, my man. When did this happen?"

"Shh!" Sam didn't want his sharks disturbed.

"Last week sometime, I guess," Aaron whispered defiantly. Tom itched to applaud him. "She's not sure."

"Did she—"

"Shh!" from the left.

"Shhhh!" from behind.

Like a little whispering could compete with the bloody shark music.

As soon as he could swim ashore, Tom would get the story firsthand. Cassandra had claimed she couldn't join in his bighearted plan because she had to meet with a new artist at the gallery. Tom was curious about the gallery.

And the artist.

Aaron didn't mind stopping at River Place, the nineteenth-century industrial center that had been renovated for upscale shops like Westbrook's. Sam objected, but he gave in when Aaron told him about a small video arcade tucked into an inconspicuous corner of the trendy premises.

Westbrook's was better than trendy. It was unique. A variety of paintings, sculptures, and even artifacts graced the rustic brick-and-old-wood space like pearls in barnacled oyster shells. Aaron introduced Tom to a slim, stylish young black woman named Sandy, who offered to help them.

"We came to see Aunt Cassie."

Who's obviously not here.

"Where's the video games?" Sam whispered to Aaron.

"Just a moment." Sandy moved toward the back of the shop. "Let me see if she's available."

Pointedly ignoring his brother's pouting, Tom made a show of browsing the shop. He wasn't really seeing anything except for the number of seconds it took Cassandra to emerge from the office, but he must have looked interested. Aaron told him he could probably get a special deal on the Inuit stone seal he was absently petting.

He quickly shoved his hands into his pockets and turned, smiling in response to the mere sound of her voice. "Since we were in the neighborhood, Aaron wanted to show me the gallery."

"I'm sorry I couldn't join you, but I'm really interested in carrying Marco's work. Come see." With a gesture, Cassandra invited him to a writing table flanked by chairs at the back of the store. There stood a green stone sculpture of something that reminded Tom of Jabba the Hutt. "What do you think?"

"What *I* think is there's no video games in this place," Sam muttered at Tom's back.

"God, you're a pest." He regressed a good ten years and blew his cool as he pulled a money clip from his pocket and slapped it into Sam's eager hand. "Knock yourself out."

Cassandra laughed. "Aaron knows where they are." With a nod she gave the boy her permission to show his guest some fun.

Then she laid her lovely fingers on the green thing and looked up at Tom with a proprietary smile. "Well?"

"What is it?"

"What *is* it? *Thomas,*" she chided.

She was patronizing—more like *matronizing*—him.

He smiled. Damn if he didn't have it coming. He shifted gears and regrooved.

"I'm just playin' with you, woman. It's a fine piece. Would I sound ignorant if I asked, who's Marco?"

"He's just getting started, but I think he shows great promise."

He glanced at the office door. "Do I get to meet him?"

"I'm sure he'd be thrilled to meet Thomas Warrior. Unfortunately, he's already left." She folded her arms and gave him that *tsk-tsk* look again. "Are you giving me attitude?"

"Yeah, I guess I am." But he wasn't making any apology. "What's this about somebody trying to break into your house?"

"Sandy," she called to her assistant. "Will you watch the floor?"

Finally, Cassandra let him into the office, which was small and strictly biz, with no closet in which to stash anyone named Marco.

Damn. Since when had he grown a jealous bone?

Behind the closed door, it was Cassandra who immediately switched gears. Yes, she thought there was something going on—someone casing or watching to try to get in—and she was a little scared.

"Why didn't you tell me?"

"You're not a policeman," she said simply.

"Fair enough." He would file that one away and figure it out later. "You're okay? Everything's okay?"

"Just a cigarette butt close to the house and some places where . . ." She shook her head quickly, as though it had suddenly occurred to her that she might be giving something away to the wrong guy. "I haven't found anything missing. I guess I've been careless lately."

"What did the cops say?"

"I didn't report it." She shrugged. "I don't even know what to report. I just know someone's been trying to get into my house."

"You said you were going to beef up your security system."

"I am; I'm looking into it."

He sat on the edge of the desk, avoiding her eyes as he asked warily, "So, do you have any suspects?"

"I'm not a cop either, Thomas."

"You don't know what to report, and you don't know what to think, and you don't know how to feel." He offered a sympathetic smile. "Woman, you're in a bad way."

"I feel as though I'm being watched sometimes. How do you report that?"

"When did it start?" He couldn't resist adding, "Since

you met me?"

"No, I . . ." Her eyes met his. It was hard to read them. Fear? Doubt? She glanced away again. "Recently."

They allowed a long moment of silence to speak for itself.

"Thomas," she began finally, "you came into my life out of nowhere. You're so unexpected, so different from anyone I've ever known. You make me feel . . ." She reached for his hand. "When you're with me, all I want is for you to stay, just a little longer. And when you leave me, I don't know where you go."

"I go home."

"I don't even know where that is, but you know where I live. It's not a secret place. You're welcome there."

"My home *is* a secret place. You wouldn't like it. It's not like where you live, a real house."

"A regular house for an ordinary woman," she said with a sweet, diffident shrug.

"I said *real*." Thomas took her other hand. Holding both, he drew her to stand squarely in front of him and leaned down, touching his forehead to hers. "You're not the only one who's in a bad way."

They stood that way for a moment, forehead to forehead, eyes closed, breathing each other's breath.

"You scare me, Thomas," she admitted softly.

"What have I done that scares you?"

"It's what I've done, and what I want that I didn't want before I met you. And the wild thoughts I've been having lately." She leaned back and met his gaze with her own frank one. "I can't put one and one together and come up with the right answer."

"Thomas Warrior tried to break into your house. Is that the right answer?"

"Of course not. Why would I think . . . It makes no sense if I'm what you want there, if I'm the reason you keep coming back."

"You're the reason I've come," he said solemnly. "You want proof, all you have to do is touch me."

"Is it the ledger drawings?" she asked. He questioned her with a look. "Is that what you want? Because it would be so much easier if—"

"You're talkin' trash now, woman. Is this the way a lady does it? The way you run your man down?"

"No. I didn't mean it that way." She squeezed his hands. "I want you to have them, Thomas. I should have let you have them to begin with."

He stood, staring at her in disbelief. "Is this a test?"

"It would be a gift."

"I'm not looking for gifts from you, Cassandra. I wasn't looking for anything from you." He still couldn't read that loaded look in her eyes. Loaded with what? "You don't believe me, do you?"

"It doesn't matter now. I want you to have them. You *should* have them, even if we weren't . . ."

"Having a thing? Doing our *thing?*" He gestured toward the framed art on the walls, a variety of her favorite *primitives*. "These things just speak to me. Isn't that the expression? I don't know why. I don't know where it comes from, but they do; they *speak* to me."

He was about to go off on a tear, and he knew it. So be it. He'd heard these crazy claims so often.

"I was a full-blooded Indian in a past life," he mocked.

"I was a chief. I did many of the deeds White Bull portrays in these drawings."

"That isn't one of the White Bulls," she said of the framed ledger drawing he pointed to.

He dismissed her literal response with an impatient gesture. "I saw these events with my own eyes. Wait! Maybe I was White Bull." He wagged an *aha* finger. "Maybe I *was* White Bull. Maybe I drew these myself."

"Not that one. The White Bulls are—"

"No, don't tell me. Let me find them myself. They *speak* to me." He pulled a file drawer open. "Did you bring them here for safe keeping? No? Yes? They're speaking from a distance." Like a madman, he opened one drawer after another. "Small voices. Over here, Thomas! Come get us!"

"They're not here, Thomas. They're—"

"Don't!" He clapped a hand over her mouth, turning her eyes as wild as his. "I tell you, they're speaking to me. Small voices rising from the misty past."

"What are you doing?" she demanded after jerking his hand away. "Stop this. I want you to have them, Thomas. Where are you going?"

He reached for the door. "The voices are telling me that I won't find it in this place. What I seek isn't here." He shrugged dramatically. "I guess it's back to the drawing board."

"I wasn't suggesting . . ." She caught his warning glance. Quietly she amended, "Maybe I was."

"Maybe it's all in your head, Cassandra. If it isn't, maybe you oughta call the police. Change your locks, get a new security system, hire a bodyguard."

"Don't, Thomas." She grabbed his arm before he could open the door. "Don't abandon Aaron. Please."

"Please?" He laughed. "Yeah, I can do that. That's all you know about me, isn't it? I sure can please."

"Don't act this way, Thomas."

"I don't *act,* baby. What you see is what you get." She was hanging on to his arms. He had the power. She had the need. "Do you want it?" he whispered.

"No." She looked up and undid him with the unwavering innocence in her eyes. "I want you, not *it*. I want more than a *thing*. I want . . ."

"What? Tell me, Cassandra."

"I want to trust you."

He backed away. "Well, that's up to you, isn't it? Until you do, we've got a thing goin' on. Easy come, easy go."

Her arms dropped to her sides as she retreated, leaving him to open the door.

"Take it easy," he said.

"Are you coming back?"

"Right now, I'm doing the going part. I'll take my brother home and leave Aaron with you. But I'll be back at the regular time. I know where I stand with him. Aaron and me, we know what we're about."

"I wanted to talk with you about his—"

"Another time." He started to leave, but he paused to offer one last heartfelt bit of advice. "Don't be afraid to call the police if somebody's messing with you, Cassandra. Let the cops do their job."

"I'm not . . ." Her final protest followed him out the door. ". . . afraid."

IT WAS A PHONE CALL FROM THE WOMAN
that gave Victor the idea to use the boy, who had ready
access to the house and to almost everything she owned.
And her words had given Victor the key to the boy—that
at his tender age he was already curious about life's dark
side.

Cassandra had fretted over her responsibility for giving the boy unrestricted access to cyberspace. She told
Thomas she had just seen a story on TV about the
graphic content on some of *those* websites, and she was
shocked. Nudity was nothing compared to "that stuff."
Thomas liked her "nudity was nothing" comment, but
she was serious. This was a serious matter, and she was
at fault. She wore blame like a crystal crown. It was all
her doing. The computer was her gift. Unrestricted
access to the knowledge of good and evil.

Was it an Apple? Victor, the consummate eavesdrop-
per, burned to ask when Thomas missed the obvious
opportunity. But Victor could only listen.

Poor, crazy Cassandra. She was crazy over Thomas.
She was crazy with fretting. She was crazy with the
notion that she could find a way to make everything all
right again, if only she could find the right way. What
should she do, Thomas? Help, Thomas! What should
this used-to-be-cool, suddenly crazy, poor little rich
woman do?

Stupid woman. Where was *her* gift of vision? She
worried about what the boy would see. She was missing

the real danger: *What* would see the boy?

Victor composed his first irresistible message.

I think you know me, Aaron. My name is
Victor. Thomas Warrior is our mutual friend.
Readers assume that I am a figment of his
imagination, but just between you and me, I'm
a lot more than his figment. It's important that
you keep this contact confidential. Do not
mention it to our mutual friend. He will deny
me, and I hate it when he does that. He
expects me to carry out his plans, but he
denies me even one true ally. Everyone needs
an ally. I wouldn't blame you if you doubted
my identity at this moment. You can't believe
everything you read, but seeing is believing.
Perhaps that can be arranged.

Victor pushed Send. He imagined the twisting path the
message must take on its way to the boy. Victory would
see to its safe and secret arrival. The boy would feel
secure in his sense of her presence, and his curiosity
would fuel the response Victor needed.

Meanwhile, Victor needed his own brand of fuel. He
would find it on the streets he knew so well, and when he
returned, he would plan his next move, for he would
have his answer from the boy.

chapter 9

"SHOW ME WHAT YOU'VE BEEN WORKING ON this week, my man."

Aaron slouched in his chair, both hands laying protectively over the portfolio on the library table. He made no move to open it.

It was going to be one of those days, Tom told himself.

"I don't have anything new," Aaron said sullenly.

"You're reworking some of the old stuff?"

"Trying to." The boy gripped the edge of the portfolio. Finally, he sighed, opened the flap, and slid one drawing into view. It was an unfinished face. "I know you think it's too violent or whatever, but when I try to take some of that out, it's, like, wimpy."

"I'm not telling you to take stuff out. I'm just telling you what I see." Tom saw erasures. He saw that his pupil had retreated from exposing a degree of anguish in the eyes and removed a scar from the neck. He glanced up and saw big blue eyes in need of something that Tom felt unqualified even to identify, much less offer.

He gave what he hoped was an encouraging smile. "It's always strictly one man's view."

"Yeah, but you're the teacher. You know best."

"Bullshit." Tom laid his hand on the boy's shoulder. "What's goin' on, Aaron?"

"Are you . . ." Aaron glanced at the far end of the table, the fireplace, finally tucked his chin, narrowing his field of vision to a small patch of his sweater. "We're cool with the Internet stuff, right?"

"What do you mean, cool?"

Tentatively, Aaron looked up. "I've been staying out of those kinds of chat rooms you were talking about. You made your point."

"I don't know that I had a point—more like a word to the wise—but it sounds to me like a wise man is making his own choices."

"Did you tell my mom?"

"Nope." *Damn, that word had a sneaky sound to it.* Before Aaron could ask about anyone else he might have told, Tom added, "Would I narc a brother over?"

"Brother?"

"We're in this together." His gesture took in pen, ink, pencils, and paint—tools of their trade. "That makes us brothers."

"On paper," Aaron concluded.

"On paper." Tom clapped his hand on the boy's shoulder, harder this time, man to man. "Which is a technicality for most people, but for us it's where we commit ourselves, heart and soul."

"Yeah," Aaron allowed softly. "Do you ever get stuck? Like you're trying to move on to something different, but you keep going back to the old ideas?"

"Sure. I was comfortable with Dark Dog. I had been repeating myself for a long time. I couldn't get any new tricks out of the ol' dog, but I felt safe with him. He was a sure thing.

"Now I'm reaching the same place again, and I'm starting to dig in my heels, you know, scared shitless to make a change. But then I ran into . . ." Tom lifted his hand in a hold-on gesture, then cocked a finger. "I gotta show you something, man. These are gonna blow you away. They did me. Come on upstairs."

Tom took the steps two at a time. He'd put the ledger-drawings lesson on the back burner, waiting for the right cue from his protégé. *Do you ever get stuck?* Magic, gut-churning words. Now that the time had come, he hoped Cassandra hadn't moved them yet. But after the show he'd put on in her office—damn, it embarrassed him to think about it—she'd be crazy not to lock them away.

He found the folio in her bedroom, in the same place he'd last touched them. Their significance to him redoubled with each viewing, and his hands had already gone clammy in anticipation. Lovingly he laid them out on the bed, extolling the virtues of each piece as he arranged them in order.

Aaron watched quietly. Finally, he exposed his twenty-first-century graphics bias.

"Are you telling me *this* would *sell?*"

Tom laughed. "You wouldn't believe what your Aunt Cassie paid for them."

"Yeah, but that's because they're old."

"It's because they're beautiful. But what I want you to look at is the way they tell a story. No words, just figures and color and movement."

"Yeah, but—"

"No words, my man. Just look."

After a time, Aaron risked a glance at his mentor.

Tom nodded. "Tell me what you see."

"I like the way he carries a detail from one picture to the next. Like this dog," Aaron observed, pointing out the figure without touching the paper.

"I think that's Coyote."

"Are you doing a new story from these?"

Tom cocked a finger at the boy and gave a right-on wink.

"But that's copying," Aaron scolded.

"*From* these. Lately I'm sitting down to my drafting table, and these drawings start to give me ideas, one tumbling over the other. It feels like the man who did these is standing right behind me, looking over my shoulder, bringing his world into mine."

"So it's still your style, but his story?"

"Maybe it's our story, his and mine. It's about our people. It's like the panels form a river that flows through us, through his time and mine. I'll do my part to carry it around another bend."

"But you're saying it's okay to use *his* story," Aaron insisted.

"My style is different. My words are contemporary, and my voice is my own. When you read my story, you'll recognize its roots, but you'll be reading a new story for a different time. It's also an old story for *all* time." Tom reached for the book that had been left on the nightstand, hoping it would help him prove his point.

But it was nonfiction. Pre-Columbian pottery. *Thanks, Cassandra.*

"Do you know how many times the Greek myths have been rewritten?" Tom asked, gesturing, book in hand. "Or Romeo and Juliet, or Cinderella? That's why storytellers are readers and listeners first. That's why you spend four days a week doing the school stuff that you claim has nothing to do with art." He gave a stern look. "It does."

"How did you get to be so smart?"

He remembered Jesse Brown Wolf telling him about the Trickster, who took a variety of shapes in Native traditions, including Old Man Coyote, who he believed had inspired the Wile E. Coyote character.

Jesse deserved some credit.

But Tom withheld it behind a smile. "I stayed in school."

"Did you go to college? Aunt Cassie says she'll pay for me to go to college."

"You're lucky. But I was lucky, too. I had a scholarship and a part-time job. Whatever it takes, if you get the chance, take it."

"But you liked school. I bet you had a lot of friends."

"I've always been my own man. Like you."

"Brothers, right? It's even okay that I'm white."

"Hey, you are, aren't you?" Tom tapped the boy's plump chest with the back of his hand. "I hardly noticed."

"Liar. Some kids call me Doughboy."

"No shit? Some kids' mothers didn't teach them much." Fortunately, Tom's had taught him to quit saying every damn thing that popped into his head.

Thanks, Angela.

"Sam's not your real brother, either, is he?" Aaron asked.

"You don't play a brother that way—disown him just because he's spoiled." Tom set about carefully replacing the ledger drawings in their case. "The Lakota say we're all related, but you and me, we have

114

the Brotherhood of the Pencil."

"Kind of like a warrior society?"

"That's what I'm talking about. I'll put these away while you go downstairs and choose your weapons. Charcoal, lead, colors, whatever fits you best. Let's put pencil to paper and see if we can't get you unstuck."

"Okay."

Aaron was halfway out the door when Tom had another thought. "You know what *Lakota* means, don't you?"

The boy shook his head.

"'Ally.' *Kola* is 'friend,' but an ally is somebody you trust with your back, you know what I'm sayin'? You won't be getting a knife in your back as long as a Lakota stands with you." Tom smiled. "We're allies, you and me."

Aaron stared at him for a moment, then swallowed hard, as though he were taking a horse pill.

"I understand."

ADVANCING THE MERITS OF TRUST SEEMED to require Tom to risk a measure of his own. Maybe he'd been a little too defensive over Cassandra's suspicions. Not that he was totally out of line, the way she'd turned him down on his generous offer of a day spent with three fine males. She had her reasons. Maybe they really did have more to do with her new "find" than with Tom. What was his name, Marco?

Tom wasn't about to start worrying about any pansy-ass named *Marco*. He wanted to hear Cassandra's voice. What did he have to lose by calling her?

"Any sign of your burglar this week?" he asked, playing it cool, cards to the chest.

"None that I've noticed," she said, seeing his cool bet with her breezy one. "No sign of my lover, either."

"Could they be one and the same?"

"Your guess would be far better than mine. All I can do is hope."

"Hope the burglar and the lover aren't the same jerk who went off on you in your office the other day?"

She laughed. "My pantry is stocked and ready for another raid."

"How about if you come over here and raid mine?"

"If I knew where you kept your pantry, I would have done that a long time ago."

He laughed and happily gave her the address. He told her to park behind the building, where he would meet her and show her the secret entrance to the secret passage to the secret stairway to his secret haven.

She was enchanted.

The top floor of Thomas's warehouse had a distant view of the best parts of the city—the skyscrapers with their crowns of colored light, the Mississippi River with its array of lighted bridges. But the immediate neighborhood was less spectacular, with its old brick warehouses, small storefronts, a few unassuming upper floors converted to pricey apartments and condos, with more to come. He told her about the charter school on the ground floor and how he'd gotten more personally involved with it lately. She gave him a you-know-better look when he added that he wasn't sure why.

His open living space was the polar opposite of her own home in almost every way she could imagine. She was south; he was north. She was a ground-nester, a grouse or a mourning dove. He was an eagle. His colors were black and white, with splashes of primary red, blue, and yellow. Wood, metal, glass, and brick surfaces had been cleaned and polished until their natural beauty radiated.

"I had a designer, if that's what you're wondering," he told her.

She stood before one of the many huge windows. It was a place that looked out, even though it didn't open out. She wasn't even certain she could find the way out, but she hardly felt closed in.

"You can see so much from here," she marveled as they watched dusk envelop the city, descending like a soft mantle over a huge catch of fireflies.

"It's the old part of the city—what used to be the industrial part—so you don't have to be twenty stories up to have a view. I get to see the old flour mill instead of the new General Mills, which is out in the 'burbs now. I need the city around me so I can soak up all the nuances. Attention to detail is my stock in trade."

She glanced toward the door. She knew where it was only because they'd walked through it, but it had now become part of the brick wall.

"I brought you up the stairs so you'd know where they are, but there's also a freight elevator," he told her. "Come choose a bottle of wine."

"What's downstairs?" she asked as she followed him

to the black and stainless steel kitchen area with its sleek, Euro-meets-retro design.

"The school has been hounding me for the second floor. I like having a substantial cushion between us, but I'll probably let them have it. I'll still have the third floor as a buffer."

At the touch of his hand, a section of black wall revealed itself to be a nearly seamless swinging door, which he held open for her as he flipped on the light.

She could have sworn she'd entered a cellar. It was at least twenty degrees cooler than the rest of the apartment. Brick gave way to stone walls lined with wine racks, pantry shelves, bookshelves—a collection of vintage books, unless her keen eye was badly mistaken—a couple of chairs, a large table.

"You could hibernate up here all winter and never go out for anything but the newspaper," she said as she set about checking wine labels.

"There shouldn't be any news in the winter," he said. "Let people stay close to the fire and take care of their families until spring."

"I like that idea, except that . . ." *What would people like me do?* She selected a bottle of chardonnay. "This looks good. Do you keep anything on the third floor?"

With a sly smile, he took the bottle from her hand. "Booty."

"Meaning loot, or . . ."

"Okay, you got me. *Bodies.*" He pushed open the black swinging door, inviting her through with a melodramatic gesture to match the villainous smile. "The corpses of characters I might need to resurrect."

"How do you sleep at night?"

"I don't. I work." He set the bottle on the kitchen counter and turned to her, back to the real Thomas again. "Those floors are sealed tight so the kids can't get up there and get into trouble. There's still some old junk down there. Furniture, doors, windows, kitchen sinks, parts of machines that only an antique dealer can recognize, all entombed."

"There's quite a market for stuff like that, now. Architectural antiques."

"Wanna go into business with me?" He handed her two wineglasses and continued to strategize while he rummaged in a drawer. "We'll get ourselves some dust masks and venture down there. Maybe we'll have an auction. A singles auction—unattached bidders only. Hey!" Eyes sparkling, he brandished a corkscrew. "We'll turn it into a TV show. What can we call it?"

" 'Who Wants to Marry a Pack Rat?' "

"Yeah, that's a good one." The downturn in his tone hinted that marriage was going a little far. "I hope you like Chinese."

"You've got a Chinese pack rat lined up for me?"

He laughed. "I was planning to whip up some stir-fry." The merriment in his eyes went soft as he touched her cheek. "After that I've got you lined up with a guy who's a lot like stir-fry. A little bit of everything, all in one pot."

"I love stir-fry."

Love? They were both going soft, standing there looking into each other's eyes like lusty, besotted teenagers.

Love was going a little far.

• • •

CASSANDRA WOKE UP ALONE IN THOMAS'S
bed. It took her a moment to get her bearings, but she
was sure it wasn't her bed. It was huge, for one thing.
It took another moment to ascertain that she was,
truly, the only one in it. And then another to realize
that she shouldn't be. Thomas ought to be sleeping
beside her. It had been a long and luscious night. They
had opened another bottle of wine after dinner, made
dizzying love by the city's nightlight, and she had
fallen asleep in his arms.

It couldn't be morning. The only light in the apartment
illuminated the desk in the far corner. Dark, heavy
drapes covered the windows. The smell of soy sauce lingered in the air. The scent of sex filled the bed, attesting
that the reason for her overall physical satisfaction—if
she disregarded the wine woozies—was not a dream.

But neither was the fact that her lover had disappeared.

His home seemed to be furnished with all the conve-
niences except a functioning clock. The digital versions
were stuck on 12:00 or 00:00. She was certain she'd left
her watch in the bathroom, but she didn't find it there.
Somehow she felt as though she was breaking house
rules when she pulled a drape aside and discovered that,
not only was it morning, but it was *late* morning.

Where was that man? Quietly disappearing when he'd
visited her bed had enhanced his mystique, but leaving
her alone in his own bed struck her as downright

unfriendly. Where was the morning coffee? Where were the cute quips and lingering looks given to put doubts to rest? *Baby, it was more than good. It was the best I've ever had.*

Baby? What was she thinking, *baby.*

Mr. Ten-Years-Her-Junior Thomas Warrior, that's what. *The hell with the morning chitchat, mama.*

Cassandra's pride would not permit her to wait patiently for his return. Someone had gathered her clothes off the floor and laid them neatly over the back of a chair near the bed. What kind of a hint was that? She dressed quickly and found her way out. To hell with all of his silly secrets, she told herself as she pushed the Down button and suffered a maddeningly slow descent on the creaky elevator.

Rude sunlight blasted Cassandra right in the eye when she emerged from the building, but she found her car where she'd left it. She'd almost expected it to be gone. She reached into her purse for her keys and found her watch there as well. She was certain—well, fairly certain—she'd left it in the bathroom.

She could almost hear someone saying, *Here are your clothes. Don't forget your watch.*

The sunlight wasn't the only thing that had been rude to her this morning. And, no, calling it rudeness wasn't going too far at all.

Cassandra didn't realize that she had company until she was halfway up her own driveway. Darcy leaped from her car and slammed the door. She pulled her jacket around her beneath folded arms and stood amid the frostbitten hostas that lined the driveway, glaring Cassandra down as she approached.

"Where have you been all night?" Darcy demanded.

Cassandra stepped out and tried to recall some promise or plan made the last time she'd spoken with her sister, but none came to mind. She lifted a hand to shade her eyes as she closed the car door behind her. "Are you your sister's keeper?"

"Don't be a smart-ass. I'm in no mood." Darcy stooped to peer through Cassandra's car windows. "Where's Aaron?"

"What do you mean?"

"He isn't anywhere else to be found." She whirled to confront and confound Cassandra. "He *has to be* with you."

"I haven't seen him for a couple of days. Didn't he come home from school yesterday?"

Darcy flapped her arms. "Apparently he didn't *go* to school yesterday."

"Stop!" Cassandra raised her hand like a traffic cop. "He's been missing since *yesterday?*"

"I got the days mixed up. I was thinking he was here for his art lessons or something. I came over to get him and no one was home, so I was sure you'd taken him out somewhere," Darcy explained, rattling on breathlessly. "So I just went ahead with my plans, but when I came home, and he wasn't there, and I called here, and there was no answer, and I went—"

"Wait a minute." The stop sign went up again. "What time did you get home?"

"It was late. What difference does it make? I thought he was with you."

"I wouldn't take him anywhere without—"

"But when I called and called and you didn't answer . . ."

"Darcy! I wouldn't take him unless—"

"He was mad at me." Darcy was on the verge of tears. "I thought maybe he came over here, and you took his side and wouldn't answer the phone or something, I don't know."

"Why was he mad at you?"

"He spoke to me disrespectfully," Darcy snapped. Cassandra pinned her younger sister to the spot with a look that demanded more. "About my social life," Darcy added defensively.

"Your latest boyfriend?"

"Cassie, I slapped him," Darcy confessed as her defensiveness gave way to desperation. "I never raise a hand to him, you know that, but he's never talked that way to me before. I'll bet it's that mentor of his. That's probably where he is, too."

"No, he isn't at Thomas's."

Darcy went still, staring in disbelief. "*That's* where you were all night?"

"Don't worry about where I was, Darcy. Worry about where Aaron—"

"He ran away," Darcy whispered, finally setting her tears loose. "Oh, my God, my baby ran away."

chapter 10

CASSANDRA HAD BEEN DARCY'S LAST HOPE.
It was time for Cassandra's wit and common sense to
pick up where Darcy's ended. They checked the house.
No Aaron. They checked the garage, the yard, the neigh-
bor's yard, calling his name, hoping he would burst forth
from the bushes. But there was to be no such opportunity
for joyous scolding. Not yet, anyway. Cassandra's
instincts told her to pile her sister into the car and keep
looking. Start with the school. They could call the police
from there and possibly find out whether he'd gotten on
the school bus, whether anyone had spoken to him or
noticed anything that might offer a clue to where he
might have gone.

But the other students gave typical angelic wags of
their heads when asked whether they had any idea where
Aaron might be.

"We'll call Jesse." Angela turned her class over to her
aide and headed for the office phone. The call was brief.
She reconfirmed times and last sightings with Angela
and Darcy, relaying each detail from the women into the
receiver.

"Jesse says he'll meet you at Darcy's house, which is
where you need to be in case Aaron comes home or tries
to call," Angela said as she hung up the phone. She
turned to Darcy. "He missed school yesterday, but you
didn't miss him until late last night?"

"I was thinking it was the day he had his art lessons,"
Darcy claimed. Angela glanced at Cassandra, who

looked away. "I don't know why, but for some reason I got the schedule mixed up," Darcy insisted. "I was running late, and I just thought he was still with Thomas. I left Aaron a note about where I was going, in case he came home."

"In case?" Angela challenged.

"We had a little disagreement." Darcy sighed as she nervously fingered the seam on her purse strap. "He always runs to Cassie when he's mad at me. But he didn't come home or call and leave a message, and he knows better than that. So when I came home and he wasn't in his bed, I started calling. Late or not, I tried to track him down. But Cassie was gone, too. When it got to be four, five A.M. and he still wasn't home, I tell you, by then I'm getting a little panicky."

"Maybe he's with Tommy," Angela suggested.

"No, Cassie was with . . ." Darcy caught herself, glanced at her sister, and shrugged. ". . . Tommy."

Angela took a moment to reduce the magnitude of her surprise so that she could pack it into one small "Oh." Then she turned somewhat coolly to Cassandra. "What does he think? Does he have any ideas?"

"Thomas left the apartment before I woke up this morning." Cassandra brightened. "I'll bet that's why he left. Maybe Aaron *is* with Thomas. If Aaron did run away and then get scared, who else would he call to come and get him?" She turned to her sister. "And he probably asked Thomas not to tell anyone. Thomas has this thing about not ratting people out." Her glance ricocheted to Angela as she added awkwardly, "So to speak."

"You've got that right," Angela said. "But he usually—"

"Does he have a cell?" Darcy asked.

"Tommy?" Angela chuckled as she snatched the receiver off the hook for another call. "He's not fond of phones. As I was about to say, he keeps the ringer turned off on his home phone most of the time," she reported as she punched the keys. "But he does check his messages." She shook her head as she thrust the phone into Cassandra's hand. "No answer, as usual. I'll leave the messaging to you."

"Thomas, it's Cassandra. If you're there, please pick up. We can't— Thomas?" She glanced at Angela, who gave her the elevated eyebrows. "I'm so glad I caught you."

Angela directed an oddly collected look at the ceiling, every bit the mother putting the son she thought she knew into an unfamiliar picture.

Relief or derision? Cassandra couldn't permit herself to dwell on Angela's current mind-set.

"Just ask him if Aaron's with him, for God's sake," Darcy demanded.

"Aaron seems to be AWOL, and we're all praying he's with you." His answer dropped from Cassandra's ear to her gut like a lead weight. She glanced from one anxious face to the other and shook her head.

"Who's *we?*" Thomas asked. "Where are you?"

"At his school with Darcy and your . . . his . . ."

"Angela," Aaron's teacher, Thomas's mother, name supplied. "How long has he been gone?" asked Thomas.

"Darcy hasn't seen him since he left the house yesterday morning. But he didn't make it to school, and he didn't come to my house, and he's not with you, and now we're really getting—"

"Jesus, that long? Have you called the police?"

"Jesse's on his way over to Darcy's, which is where we're going right now, but we were hoping . . . Thomas, has Aaron said anything to you about—"

"Hold the questions," Thomas said. "Tell me how to get to Darcy's. I'll meet you there."

JESSE BROWN WOLF STUDIED THE FACE OF the boy in the photograph he'd carried back to his office to compare with incoming reports. But nothing had been called in—no boy fitting his description found alive or dead.

Aaron Farmer didn't look much like the kids whose pictures typically made their way to Jesse's desk. But there was no telling a kid by his looks. Nobody knew that better than a juvenile officer. A twelve-year-old kid's face was his best cover.

This one looked like—how had Sammy described him? A chunky, blond version of Harry Potter. It was a reference his son figured Dad would "get" since they'd seen the movie together. What he *got* was that Aaron was not Sammy's budding notion of cool.

The boy sure as hell didn't fit the profile for a runaway. From what he'd gathered in what had to be the strangest interview he'd ever had—the witnesses being the boy's flakey mom, who had the hots for every man who had a pulse; his own son, who could barely stand to be in the room with his father; and the boy's aunt, whose presence in the same room with Jesse's son visually defined the old expression that two people were "sparking." Then along came the boy's teacher, who happened to be Jesse's wife and the aunt's friend, and man! The room was so charged with complicated relationships that Jesse had some serious trouble focusing on the fact that a kid was missing. Which was why he couldn't get himself off the case fast enough.

But there was no way he could stay out of it, not completely. The kid mattered to people who mattered to him.

"Aaron is a very sensitive person," the kid's mother had claimed. "I know I hurt his feelings. He said some things about this guy I've been seeing, and I got mad, you know? Because, for one thing, it just wasn't like Aaron to talk to me like that." She shot an accusatory glance at Tom. "So I told him that if he didn't stop hanging on to me, people would be calling him a mama's boy along with everything else."

"Everything else?"

"He gets teased, Cassie, you know that. But I won't have him talking to me that way. I *am* his mother." The woman was obviously holding something back. "Okay, I slapped him," she conceded. "Not hard, but I did slap his face. I admit it." She squared up as she turned to Jesse. "It's not like him to sass me, and it's not like me to hit him. But I did. I admit it."

From the position he'd taken at the front window, Tom eyed his father. "You gotta be careful what you say to a cop, Darcy."

"I'm here because your mother called me," Jesse told him. "I'm trying to help, not kick ass and take names."

"I can tell you, from what I know of Aaron, he's not an abused kid," Tom reported as he turned back to keeping watch.

"Where's his father?" Jesse asked Darcy. "Have you called him?"

"I lost touch with him long ago. He hasn't been around since Aaron was a baby."

"We'll track him down."

"Oh, God," Darcy said with a bitter groan. "There's no way. Really. Daryl Anderson is *so* out of the picture."

Jesse jotted down the name. "It would have to be Anderson. Last known address and place of employment?"

"We lived in Wisconsin." She reached for Jesse's pen. "Here, I'll write it down for you."

"And the guy you and Aaron had the argument about?"

"I didn't tell Rory about the argument."

"That's not the point, Darce," Cassandra put in. "Just write it down."

"Another one bites the dust," Darcy muttered as she printed the name on Jesse's pad. "No great loss."

"What about Aaron's friends? Could he be off with another kid?" Jesse found himself searching nearly blank female faces. A little sadness, a little guilt, a big empty.

"No friends?"

"None his age, really," Darcy said quietly. "He used to play with other children when he was little, but the things he likes to do now don't lend themselves to social—"

"He gets along better with adults," Cassandra said.

"He's shy. He's not involved in many activities. He's . . ." Darcy sighed. "No friends."

The picture they painted was becoming way too pitiful to take, even for a cop. Jesse cast about for a liberating comment. "Friends can cause trouble, too, you know. It's a double-sided coin."

"I can't imagine where he stayed last night. What was the temperature last night? Did it hit freezing? He was only wearing . . ." Darcy leaned toward Jesse's notes. "I already told you that, didn't I?"

"Lightweight brown jacket, blue and white sweater, brown pants." He hated seeing the anguish in a mother's face when they discussed a child's clothing. When he'd asked Darcy to supply him with something Aaron had worn, she'd brought him a plaid sweater, cradling it in her hands as though it might have been his favorite.

No wonder the kid couldn't make the cut for cool.

"I can't imagine him running away," Cassandra said.

"Maybe he went to your house," Darcy suggested to her sister. "But since you were *gone all night*—"

"Aaron has a key."

"Don't beat yourselves up with if-onlys. I'll go back downtown and get this information into the system right away. We'll get out an Amber Alert. You need to stay by the phone," Jesse told the boy's mother, and to Tom he said, "If you think of anything that might help . . ."

"You want me to draw you a picture?"

Give it a break, Jesse warned his son with a sharp

look. But for the sake of civility, he said, "I've got a picture."

And Jesse was studying it when Tom appeared at the door of his tiny office at the police station. Thomas Warrior. Tom Little Warrior. Tommy T.

Jesse Brown Wolf's son.

Tom's earlier sarcasm had made reference to a time when he had drawn pictures to help Jesse identify thugs who had been making trouble around the playground at Tommy T's school. His remarkable talent had been evident then, and the drawing had been the key to busting a drug ring.

"Come on in." Jesse nodded toward an armless chair. "Remember the first time you came to my door?"

"You mean your hole in the ground?" Tom straddled the chair, resting his arms across the back. "You weren't so cordial then. You made me sit outside."

"My headaches were pretty bad back then." The pain had, in fact, all but consumed him. "You were respectful of my privacy. You stayed up there where you belonged, where you couldn't see my face, and you talked to me. It was a good arrangement, under the circumstances. The only one I could tolerate."

"You want me to stand outside the door here and say what I came to say?"

"I was remembering. That's all, just remembering that first night." Jesse leaned back in his swivel chair. "Do you ever think about what it was like then? You living on the streets and me living in a hole in the ground? It's kind of hard to believe it was real, isn't it? I mean, with all we've got going for us now."

"I didn't come here to talk over old times."

"You came to tell me what you know about a kid who's lonely and needed a friend and lucked out when he found you."

"When did you turn all sentimental?"

Jesse chuckled. "Fatherhood does it to you."

"You were a father before I came along." It was a reference to the two children Jesse had had with his first wife. His daughter was grown now, her memories of accidentally shooting her baby brother with her father's service pistol finally put to rest. The look in Tom's eyes turned soft. "I'm sorry. I shouldn't be going there."

"You can go there anytime. I do, and I go in peace these days."

"Thanks be to God," Tom said sarcastically.

With a look, Jesse finally got him to give a small chuckle. "Peace?"

"Yeah, truce. Let's find this kid. He's a misfit, like me."

"You were never a misfit. Everyone liked you." Jesse smiled fondly. "You were always looking out for people."

"Yeah, well, I gave up on that effort right about the time you busted my brother."

"You said truce."

"Right." Tom took a deep breath and got back on course. "And you're right about Aaron being a loner, but I can't see him running."

"He doesn't look like a runner."

"Come on, Jess. You've put on a few pounds yourself."

Jesse smiled and patted his stomach, which he would have defended as lovingly fed, although hardly out of control, but he welcomed Tom's ribbing. It had been too long.

"No lie," Tom continued, "this kid doesn't go anywhere unless it's with Cassandra, or lately with me. He wears two house keys on a chain around his neck, and if he's not in school, he's at one house or the other."

"Has he been to your place?"

"No. He has no idea where it is."

Jesse nodded. He could always tell when Tom was holding back on something he considered distasteful. "So, what else?"

"He's into some pretty dark stuff on the Internet. Vampires, cannibals, body parts, stuff like that."

"We'll pick up the computer." He picked up a pencil and added *computer* to his notes on this case that wasn't his.

"He wants to do comic books, and he's good. I mean, that's why I hooked up with him, because he's got real talent." Tom shook his head. "But he sure has some scary images floating around in his young head."

"Didn't you?"

"I didn't have the Internet."

"You had the streets."

"All right, man, I know how it works, and so do you. I could have gone down that road along with my brother. That's what you're saying."

"We're talking about Aaron Farmer. We're figuring out what's in *his* head and where it might have taken him. If it had been you, you might have hit the streets."

"Right." Tom rested his chin on fists stacked on the back of the chair. "Not this kid."

"You're thinking somebody picked him up."

Tom closed his eyes. Muscles twitched in his jaw.

Jesse knew where Tom's head was, and what that photographic imagination of his could do to him. "Don't, Tom. It won't do any good."

"It might. You start with 'what if,' you take it step by step, you see where it leads."

"It's not the same as a character in one of your stories. You're starting with a real kid."

"You do that all the time."

"This kid is part of your life. You're imagining the worst, and you're letting it—"

"I need to figure out where it leads, Jess. His mom is wrong about friends. He has one. He has a friend who knows him pretty well." Tom bit his lower lip, finally shook his head again. "Aaron didn't run away."

"Does Cassandra agree with your assessment?"

"I haven't talked with her about it yet. I left her sister's right after you did." He sighed. "So I wouldn't have to talk with her about it yet. Chickenshit, I guess."

"You came to the right place, Tom." Jesse reached over to squeeze his son's shoulder, relieved when he didn't flinch at the gesture. "You're talking to the right man."

"I hope so."

THE BOY'S BODY LAY LIKE A PUPPET WITH broken strings, on a pile of knocked-down cardboard boxes.

"What have you done now, you fool?" Victory demanded in her clumsy counterpart's ear.

Victor lifted his spoils aloft. "I have the key to the house."

"He's only a boy."

"It was the only way."

"It was the easy way. You took the easy way, Victor. I don't condone this. Thomas certainly does not condone this. There was no instruction for this, no plan. We've never done anything like this."

"Thomas has never been involved the way he is this time," Victor protested, seemingly speaking to great shadows cast against the cold walls. "I had to find a fool-proof way to get inside the house."

"You've proved your foolishness, but at least you've found a way," Victory said, but the limp body of an innocent child obviously displeased her. "What will you do with him?"

"I haven't decided." Victor squatted next to the cardboard mattress, clasping his hands between his knees as he studied the boy's face. They shared commonalities, he and this boy. They loved the stories. They believed. They would sacrifice their own safety in the interest of a greater need.

Victor spoke over his shoulder. "It looks bad for

me, doesn't it?"

"You must be the only one."

"Yes, I know."

chapter 11

CASSANDRA FOUGHT HER WAY BACK FROM A
night of drugged dreaming. It was like slogging through
swamp water toward something, someplace somewhat
lighter. It would be easy to sink back, but sooner or later
the effort had to be made. The heaviness was all.

She emerged from the dark tunnel with eyes that
wouldn't focus immediately, and when they did, she was
staring at meaningless words on the spine of a book. Did
pottery have anything to do with the dull dread crowding
around her head? Or was history bothering her? Pre-
Columbian days, pre–sleeping pills, pre-pre-yesterday.

*Make the last three days go away. They never hap-
pened. Call Aaron, go pick him up, don't let him out of
your sight for a week.*

There's the phone, she told her arm, waiting right
there between the book and the glass of water. Reach for
it. Dial the number. *Hey, it's Aunt Cassie.*

There's the unblinking phone.

Cassandra rolled to her back and stared at the ceiling.
There was no help to be found in separating nightmare
from reality when one was no better than the other. The
unthinkable weighed heavily, even in daylight. The
phone had not rung.

She pushed herself off the bed, fumbled for her robe, and froze mid-reach. The rarely used armoire doors stood ajar. She flew to the cabinet, envisioning the empty drawer even before she opened it.

The ledger drawings were gone.

You're not a cop, she reminded herself. Stay calm. Get dressed. Don't touch anything. Don't think.

The latter admonition was unnecessary. Her brain had become a blender, spinning reason into mush.

Cassandra searched the house for signs of a break-in and found none. The doors and windows were still locked. Nothing was broken. As far as she could tell, nothing had been moved. Had the thief closed the armoire properly, the theft of the ledger drawing might have gone unnoticed for days, weeks.

She picked up the phone.

She put it down again. Stupid woman. She had yet to call her insurance agent about the ledger drawings. They might not even be covered. Not that he was the first person she needed to report to now, but he would be the easiest to talk to at the moment. It would be a simple business call. *Does my umbrella policy automatically cover new acquisitions?* She wouldn't have to mention the unmentionable. She could speak as though she were still in control of her life and pretend that nothing had changed.

Get on with it. She picked up the phone again and got as far as dialing the nine.

Again, she put the phone down. More policemen searching the house, asking questions, taking notes, asking more questions. Who? What? Where? When? How?

Why? Unwelcome answers eddied around one person. He wanted the drawings. He knew where they were. Maybe he suspected that last night would be a good time to rip them off.

But she had offered to give them to him. Why would he steal them? Was he playing games with her?

She was reaching for the phone when it rang. She snatched it up, mid-ring. "Hel—"

"Cassie, you haven't heard from Aaron, have you?"

"Oh, Darcy, I wish I could say I had." As long as there was no tragedy to report, it was good to hear her sister's voice.

"Or the police?"

"I haven't heard anything," Cassandra assured her.

"I was getting ready to call them, but it's probably useless, right? They'll call me, won't they? But maybe not right away if it's bad. I'm afraid to turn on the news or leave the house."

"I am, too." Cassandra glanced at the black television screen and imagined a reporter's voice saying something about an identity being withheld until the family had been notified. Parents all over the viewing area would be counting heads. Others would be shaking heads, wondering why parents these days couldn't keep better track of their kids. *Getting ready to call the police* rang a bell. About what? The theft of a few drawings? So what?

"You shouldn't be alone," Cassandra told her sister.

"I wish I could go to work today. Does that sound terrible? I can't stand this waiting."

"What about what's-his-name? Rory?"

"What about what's-her-name, Cassie?"

"I can have my calls forwarded there. But if he ran away, he might come back here. I don't know whether—"

"What do you mean, *if?* Of course he ran away. And he probably *would* go there." After a pause, Darcy asked shyly, "You'd call me, wouldn't you?"

"You know I would."

"Even if he said not to? If he doesn't want to come home right away, tell him that's okay."

"He's not here, Darcy. I'd give anything to have him here, but he's not, and I'm really scared, too."

"You don't sound it." Darcy pouted. "You're always so infuriatingly composed, Cassie." Another pause, and she brightened. "You think he's just trying to scare me? Because if he is, he's not getting away with it. When he gets home, he's going to be grounded until he graduates from high school."

"I don't blame you. Once you get him home, it'll be hard to let him out of your sight."

"No kidding. God, I hate this waiting."

"You're smoking, aren't you?" Stupid question, Cassandra told herself. She could hear the telltale sounds.

"This wouldn't be a good time to nag, Cassie."

"You're right, it isn't. I'm sorry. I just hate for you to get started again."

"You apologize, and then you start in again. You might as well know, I never gave it up completely. When I need one, I have one. It's not that often." Darcy drew a long drag and blew it into the phone. "You're not my mother, Cassie."

Cassandra had run out of rejoinders. The smoking

remark was her poor attempt to help her sister stay on the right side. Wasn't there an old song with those sentiments? Stay on the right side of the road, and all will be well. No one can hurt a person who's on the right side. You're safe there. Those are the rules.

"Cassie?"

"I'm here."

"You'd be a good mother. Not to me, mind you, but to a child of your own. You'd be totally responsible, right on top of everything."

Like she was on top of the Internet stuff? She'd given him that blasted computer, along with Internet access—something she knew virtually nothing about.

"You're a good mother, Darcy."

"You're a lousy liar, Cassie. If Aaron could choose his own mother, it would be you, and you know it."

"He's at that age. Besides, being an aunt is like being a weekend father. I get to spoil him and then send him back to you."

"I wasn't cut out to have kids." Darcy sighed. "Although I seem to be able to make them easy enough. Why is that? Why do I get pregnant if I forget one damn pill, while fertility clinics charge some women a fortune for whatever it is they do with their test tubes to get them pregnant."

"I don't know, Darcy. I just know that we're lucky to have Aaron."

"God, you sound so pious. Aaron was lucky, right? Lucky I didn't—"

"Please, let's not do this, Darcy. Not now." Cassandra gripped the blocky phone receiver, using it to massage her temple, a mortar to pulverize her sister's ups and downs into something smooth, easy to digest.

Which would not be the jerky little gasps at the other end of the line.

"Darcy?"

"I'm here."

But she was crying. One thing they had in common was the rarity of their tears.

"Are you pregnant?"

"No."

Were you? she was on the verge of asking.

Let's not do this now, Cassandra. Your timing is no better than your sister's, and nobody asked for your judgment.

"I just have one thing to take care of, and then I'm coming over. I'll have my calls—"

"No," Darcy burbled. "I'll have my calls forwarded to your number."

"You want to come here?"

"I want to go to work. Will you stay by the phone, Cassie? Will you do that for me?"

"If that's what you want," Cassandra said quietly. The heat born of comeuppance crept into her cheeks, and her throat stung.

"I can't stand not being able to do anything but wait. If I'm with you and worrying about Aaron, I'm thinking about all my shortcomings. If I'm at work, I'm busy. I'm not thinking."

"Do you want to take my cell phone?"

"If there's any word, you know where to find me."

Cassandra stared at the phone again. Fine. No problem. She didn't want Darcy to be sitting home alone, and it made perfect sense for her to go to work. If they got together, they could do no less than talk—someone was bound to tread on a raw nerve—and no more than what Cassandra was doing right now. And wasn't there an old saying about a watched phone never ringing?

But a dialed phone did. It rang and rang, and she prayed that someone who didn't want her sitting home alone would answer.

And he did.

"Thomas, it's me."

"Hello, you," he said gently. "Any word?"

"No."

"How're you holding up?"

"Okay."

"You want some company?"

"I do, yes, but . . ." It was hard to hear his voice and hold herself in a place separate from her feelings for him.

"But what? You wanna see me or not?"

"I want to see you. I really need to . . . see you. Can you come now?"

HE RANG THE BELL. FOR GOOD MEASURE, he then pounded on the door. She'd sounded bereft, and he couldn't get to her fast enough. When the door opened, he pushed past it, grabbed her and held her, meeting his own need as much as hers. He needed to be needed, always had, but by this woman most especially. She was not needy. She wanted for nothing, but she wanted and needed him. She had told him as much, and she showed him how much in the way she held him hard and fast.

"Has something happened?"

She nodded against his shoulder.

"To Aaron?"

"No." She pressed her face against the side of his neck and whispered, "Please, God, no."

"It's okay, baby." He rubbed her long, slender back. "I'm here. Tell me what's going on."

"The waiting."

She lifted her head and drew away from him reluctantly. He expected to see some sign of tears. There was none.

"It's hard," he said quietly. "You want me to call Jesse?"

"No. There's something else that's happened." She turned her back to him, as though something about him was suddenly hard on her eyes.

"What?" Against his better judgment, he reached for her. "Cassandra, give it up. Let me help."

"Someone got into my house last night."

"Someone broke in?" He turned her, made her face him. More importantly, he searched her face. "Did he hurt you?"

"No, I'm okay. Somehow, sometime during the night, someone came in."

"Broke in, or—"

"Someone took the ledger drawings."

"How did they get in?" he insisted.

"I don't know."

"Did they take anything else?"

"I don't think so." She stared into his eyes, *through* his eyes, probing him as she told him tonelessly, "He came into my bedroom while I slept."

"They were still in your bedroom?"

"The armoire." She gestured toward the stairs. "I noticed the doors, left open just enough so that I knew that something wasn't right."

"Are you sure it happened last night? I showed the drawings to Aaron. He knew where they were."

Turning on him, she scowled askance. "You think Aaron took them?"

"I think whoever has the drawings might have Aaron." He strode to the kitchen and grabbed the phone.

"What are you doing?" She grabbed his arm. "Thomas, the drawings were there yesterday, and Aaron was gone. Now they're gone, and he's still gone, and . . ." The air around them grew heavy, and the look that passed between them stung them both. "I said you could have them," she reminded him quietly.

"Are we back to that?"

"Thomas, the doors, the windows . . ." She shook her head, tears finally welling in her eyes. "He didn't break in. He *came* in and took the drawings."

"And how would I do that, Cassandra?"

"I don't know." She looked down at the phone in his hand. "I haven't called the police yet."

"Why not?"

"Thomas, I wanted you to have them," she whispered sadly. "They were a gift."

He went all hot and sick inside, but he covered by star-

144

ing at her, mentally pinning her to her paper gift as he thumbed three buttons on the phone. Her brow creased, betraying her sudden lack of answers, and her hand slid away from his arm.

"We want to report a burglary," he told the 911 operator.

chapter 12

"WE JUST GOT ANOTHER CALL FROM YOUR son, Dog."

Murphy loved to get the drop on Jesse when he was deep in thought with his back to the door. The old gunfighter response amused Murphy greatly. The pesky cop wouldn't have been laughing if the gun Jesse wasn't carrying had been pointed at his paunch.

"Sun dog," Murphy repeated, just to make sure Jesse caught his inadvertent cleverness. "What is that, anyway? A dog that howls at the sun?" He laughed. "Yeowww! Close the blinds, bitch!"

Jesse shook his head, but he couldn't hold back on a lopsided smile. "You've got something to tell me, Murphy?"

"A burglary on Lake of the Isles. That isn't Tom's neighborhood, is it?"

Jesse's smile dropped away. "Cassandra Westbrook's place?"

"Friend of yours?"

"Friend of Angela's and, uh . . . Tom's."

"He was the one who made the call."

"Are you taking it?" Jesse was on his feet, ready to hop on board.

"Been there and done that. You won't believe what was ripped off." Murphy handed Jesse a clipboard, jabbing his finger at the important lines. "Native American artifacts. Just like in Tom's last book. Only this time it was some old drawings. Ledger drawings, they called them. Do you know about ledger drawings?"

"Yeah, Murph, I know something about ledger drawings. How did the perp get in the house?"

"We haven't figured that out yet. No sign of a break-in. Nothing else was disturbed, not even the owner. She thinks it happened during the night while she slept." Murphy elbowed Jesse's arm. "Get this. She kept the drawings in her bedroom. The perp got in and out right under her sleeping nose."

"Damn." Jesse scanned Murphy's block-print notes. "Her nephew went missing a couple of days ago."

"The kid who has a key to the house, I know. I figure it's him or whoever he's with."

"Or whoever has him."

"What's going on with that? Any leads?"

"It's not my case, but I'm keeping close tabs, and nobody's turned anything up. The mother thinks he ran because she hit him. Tom says he's not the running kind. They turned the kid's computer over to the Geek Squad. Tom thinks maybe he hooked up with some Internet perv."

"Which doesn't fit with an art heist," Murphy said. "Our guy has to know something about this kind of art and how to get it onto the world market. You can't just walk into a pawn shop with museum-quality artifacts."

"So scrap the perv," Jesse suggested. "Your guy goes after the kid to get him into the house. But why didn't he take anything else? The woman is a collector, a rich young widow. She owns a gallery."

"And her house is full of valuable art," Murphy acknowledged. "I couldn't tell you much about what I saw there except that it's worth plenty. But maybe he didn't want to leave any empty spaces on the wall, you know what I'm saying? She said herself she might not have missed the drawings if he hadn't left the cabinet door open."

"Maybe something spooked him and he took off before he was finished," Jesse suggested.

"Hell, yeah, he got in so easy, maybe he'll go back for another load."

Jesse nodded thoughtfully. "And take us to the boy."

"Is this rich bitch Tom's woman?"

Jesse answered with a cautionary glance.

"Don't give me attitude, Dog. It *is* my business."

"Yeah, well, it's none of mine."

CASSANDRA AND DARCY HAD AGREED TO take turns sitting by the phone. Cassandra understood that Darcy felt as helpless as she did, but they used their "off" times differently. Darcy went to work, using the department store hubbub to take her mind off the maddening helplessness and keep herself sane. She hadn't told anyone about Aaron's disappearance except her supervisor.

But helplessness was anathema to Cassandra. It was an intolerable state of mind. She couldn't put a crisis out of her mind, and she couldn't think about it without trying to do something. When she was sitting by the phone, it was almost impossible to keep her hands off it. Who could she call? Who might know something? Shouldn't the police have something to report by now? Were they working on the case or not?

When Darcy called to say that she had left work early, Cassandra checked her watch. She still had time to get to the school before the students were dismissed. She was convinced that there were questions that had not been asked, little stones the police were carelessly leaving unturned.

She checked in at the small school's one-woman office and then walked right into Angela's classroom, interrupting her geography lesson.

"Excuse me, Mrs. Brown Wolf. This will only take a moment. I'm wondering whether Aaron ever said anything to any of the other students. . . ." She turned to address the class. "Aaron is my nephew, and, of course, I'm getting pretty worried about him. I was wondering whether any of you can remember him saying anything at all about places he liked to go, anything that might help us find him."

"The police have already talked with us, Mrs. Westbrook," Angela said quietly. But she laid her nearly new stick of chalk carefully in the chalk tray, tugged on the map of South America and let it roll out of sight, brushed her hands together and reclaimed her class's attention.

"Has anyone thought of anything Aaron said that might give us a clue about where he went?"

More angelic silence. The children's desks were arranged in small groups of three or four. Cassandra wondered where Aaron would have been sitting.

"Your school is nice and small," she coaxed. "It's a special program for talented students, all of you so bright and perceptive. This must be like one big family with lots of brothers and sisters."

"Mrs. Westbrook, we all understand—"

"I know you do," Cassandra said with a gesture inclusive of everyone but Angela, who was obviously uncomfortable with Cassandra's persistence. "And I'm sure you're all worried about Aaron, but maybe you've been sworn to secrecy, right? Brothers and sisters do that. I know how my sister and I would tell on each other every chance we got, but if she ever told me a secret and made me promise not to tell—"

"Cassandra, we've all been interviewed," Angela said calmly. "We're not going to hold back on any secrets that might help the police find Aaron."

"Okay, but sometimes you see or hear something that you don't think anything of at the time. Like maybe you saw him talking to someone, or maybe you saw him get off the bus when he wasn't supposed to. Maybe Sam remembers something from the time they went to the museum with Thomas," Cassandra suggested eagerly, singling out Angela's son.

Sam scrunched his shoulders up to ear level. If he'd been a turtle, his head would have gone the way of the map of South America.

He stared at the book on his desk. "I was hangin' with my brother. I think we had to take Aaron because maybe it was his mentoring day or something. He didn't say much."

"How about when you all stopped in at my gallery? Maybe Aaron said something when you went off to play video games."

"All we did was play a few games. We weren't there very long." He glanced up at her. "He likes it there a lot."

"That's a good lead," Cassandra enthused. "I'm glad you mentioned it."

"I told my dad already."

"But that's something I hadn't thought of, so I appreciate your telling me."

"We're going to take the children out to the bus now," Angela said. "You can wait, or . . ."

"May I go with you? Maybe someone will think of something. If anyone thinks of anything at all, please, please tell Mrs. Brown Wolf."

Cassandra stood aside while Angela lined the children up for an orderly dismissal. The line was one child short, but she had a terrible feeling that she was the only one who noticed. The school day would follow its regular schedule until the students were told to close their books for the day, even though Aaron's chair had been empty and his books had gone unopened. The children jostled in line, as they surely did every day, but today some of them sneaked a glance at the visitor who had introduced herself as Aaron Farmer's aunt—she might have said Wolfgang Mozart's aunt for all the response she got—watching for another strange move from her, another weird speech.

"We're trying to be extra vigilant without scaring the kids too much more," Angela confided as she and Cassandra followed the line down a short hall toward the front door. "But, here, let's duck into the office. Mr. Richard," she called out to the aide at the head of the line. A signal and a nod between the two left Angela free to move Cassandra into a private space, where she obviously would have preferred the entire meeting had taken place.

"I'm sorry for the interruption, but I can't help thinking that a child can't just—" Cassandra gestured toward the children, filing through the door like a row of ducks. "He can't drop out of line without leaving a hole. There's no one who's close to him, plays with him sometimes?"

Angela closed the door behind them, but she didn't sit down. Clearly this would be a short chat. "It's hard to get Aaron to go outside and play," she explained. "He'd rather stay in and draw."

"I know he's a loner, but I didn't realize that it was this serious. Why does it take something like this?"

"How's his mom holding up?"

"She's trying to keep it together."

Angela dropped her tone to a guarded register. "How about Tommy?"

"He came over this morning."

"I didn't realize *that* was this serious." She folded her arms. "You do realize that he's not quite thirty years old."

"And I'm not quite forty." Cassandra met Angela's

gaze, woman to woman. "In case you were wondering."

"I guess it doesn't surprise me, knowing Tommy." Angela conceded, dropping the stiff pose and tone. "For some reason it's a little hard to accept."

"Me, or my age?"

"The difference in your ages. How serious is . . ." Angela touched Cassandra's arm. "I'm sorry. I don't mean to interrogate you at a time like this. I should be asking him."

Cassandra stepped back, but she offered a smile. "I'll bet it was quite a challenge, adopting a teenager off the streets. It must have been a big adjustment for both of you."

"He was close to Aaron's age, actually. Still young enough to change some of the habits that needed changing."

"How did he survive without a home?"

"By his wits," Angela said. "Which are, as I'm sure you know, very quick."

"Gifted kids can become excellent criminals. Isn't that what you told me when we were talking about getting Aaron into the mentor program?"

"I probably did, but you were just asking about Tommy. There's a difference between doing what you have to do to get by and becoming a criminal." Angela squared up and folded her arms again. "What are you suggesting?"

"You remember how Thomas and I met."

"At an auction."

"We were bidding on the same collection of draw-ings."

"You won the bid, and you have the drawings."

"Not anymore. They were stolen from my house last night."

Cassandra withstood the silence uneasily.

"And you think Tommy took them?" Angela's quiet outrage turned the indictment on Cassandra.

"I offered to give them to him as a gift, but he refused." Cassandra's throat burned with tears of frustration that she would not shed. Here was a woman who knew her lover better than she did, who could reassure her or discourage her with whatever knowledge she chose to share. "Could he be playing some kind of a game?" Cassandra asked hopefully.

"I said he was young. I didn't say he was immature," Angela snapped. "Of course he wouldn't be playing games with you right now. Did you report this theft?"

"Thomas reported it. I told him about it this morning when he came to my house. He called the police."

"There's your answer."

"I was afraid to report it." Cassandra drew a deep breath and glanced away. "When I try to put the pieces together, they only fit when I allow for unacceptable possibilities."

"I won't listen to this. Unacceptable doesn't begin to describe what you're getting out of all this. It's outrageous. Tommy is the most . . ." Angela grabbed Cassandra's arm, demanding eye contact. When she had it, she bit out, "You don't know my son."

"Not the way you do," Cassandra said softly, working hard to save face, keep it from crumpling. "But I know how I feel about him."

"Don't tell me." Angela protested needlessly with a raised palm. "I don't want to know." But she had her hunch. "How can you profess to care about him and then accuse him of stealing from you?"

"I haven't accused him of anything."

"Does he seem like the kind of person who would—"

"No, he doesn't!" Cassandra backed away. "He's been so good to Aaron."

"What are you getting at now?" Angela didn't wait for an answer that neither of them wanted aired. "You don't know my son, but I do. I don't care how your pieces fit together, Cassandra. They do not form a picture of Tommy taking your precious drawings or harming that boy."

"I don't believe it, either," Cassandra said quietly. She felt awful and ugly, and she wanted to be as good and as beautiful as Angela looked to her now—the loyal mother, the guardian angel.

But she wasn't.

"In my heart, I don't believe it," she amended, "but in my head, I'm all messed up. I don't know what to think."

"Think about letting the police do the investigating." Arms folded, Angela became the brick-wall mother. "Think about getting out of my son's life."

elsewhere

"I SEE THAT MY GUEST IS BACK AMONG the living."

Victor tipped the flashlight to relieve the boy's eyes and observed in them the gradual awakening from peace to panic.

"No, don't fight," Victor warned as the boy began to strain against his bonds. "It's only duct tape—the tape with a thousand uses, and saving your life is surely one of them."

The tape squeezed the boy's cheeks into two plump pillows under his unblinking, pale blue eyes.

"How can it be a lifesaver? you're asking me. Right now, it saves you from making the biggest mistake of your life, which would be to make any loud noise. Loud noises hurt me, and hurting me would be fatal to you."

The boy merely stared at him.

"And because we are allies, neither of us wants to hurt the other. Lakota, remember? Allies. My dream is *wolakota,* which is peace. A peaceful world, where the dignity of every person is appreciated—that would be excellent."

Victor propped his head on his arm and leaned on a tall crate containing, he was certain, only God knew what. "They talk about family values. I speak of the human family. You would not consign a member of your family to a place like this, would you?"

The boy's eyes shifted left to right, and then back to his captor.

"No, you wouldn't. You see? We are brothers, you and me. I gave you my best chair."

The boy strained against the tape, which Victor had wrapped under the tattered overstuffed chair and across the boy's lap, adding a loop around each of the boy's wrists to affix them to the arms of the chair.

"You'll make it tighter if you don't quit doing that," Victor warned. Then he chuckled. "I sound like an older brother, don't I? I will have to train you for our missions, of course. Until I have confidence in your loyalty, you'll have to tolerate trusty Mr. Duct Tape. Our tool kit on a roll."

The boy dropped his head back against the chair and stared. His arms and legs quivered visibly.

"How will you earn my confidence, you ask? Young warriors are given ample opportunity to prove themselves." Victor lifted an instructional finger. "The most common mistake for a young warrior is to ejaculate prematurely."

Victor would not have thought it possible for the boy's eyes to widen any more, but they did.

"I see that your special school for especially promising children offers some kind of sex education. Relax, my young protégé." He squatted beside the chair and leaned close to the boy's ear. "That's not what I meant."

The boy whimpered. Victor's proximity counteracted his reassurances.

"What? You don't believe me? But we're brothers." He laid a gloved hand on the boy's arm. "You must take me at my word if you hope to earn my confidence. What did I tell you about human family values? We are brothers. I would never use you in that way. It is a terrible degradation, my friend. I hope you will never know how terrible." He turned his palm up. "Certainly not at my hand. Do you believe me?"

The boy nodded.

"If I have to kill you, I will do it quickly. You will feel pain only if you struggle." He patted the boy's plump shoulder. "But I will *not ever* shame you by using you in that way. Do you trust me?"

Wide-eyed, the boy offered no response.

"Fair enough. Trust is something I'll have to earn." Victor sat on the floor beside the chair, adjusting the coyote face he had fashioned from a collection of pelts. "Now, we were speaking of premature ejaculation as it applies to a raid. The inexperienced warrior is prone to expose himself and lose the advantage of surprise by . . ."

He had to laugh. He knew it made him look like a mad fool, but he couldn't help himself. It was all he could do to keep the sound from erupting from his mouth instead of puffing through his nose.

"All right, all right." He got hold of himself and waved the nonsense away. "Another of my little jokes. I'm sorry, little brother, but it's part of my nature. You've read Thomas's stories. What do you know about Victor?"

He paused, as though his pupil might find some way to answer.

"Let me rephrase. What do you know about the Trickster? He is a joker, isn't he? He tells jokes, and he plays tricks, and sometimes he tricks no one but himself. Now here I am, in the flesh, and you see that what you have read and possibly heard is actually true.

"But you must also remember that I have two sides. I am a changeling. I don't actually see Victory, but she speaks to me. The three of us are one, you know. There is

Thomas, who created us and gives us direction; Victory, who inspires us; and I am Victor, who does what must be done to set things right.

"I make many mistakes. I have made many mistakes in the past, and who knows how many more I have in store? That's why I could use an ally. Someone who is as clever and as pure as you are. You won't be corrupted by devious so-called friends. You don't have any." Victor smiled. "You don't need them, do you?"

The boy shook his head.

"All you need is an ally and a mission. I'll give you both." He patted the boy's knee. "Now, to finish my account of the novice warrior, he is apt to be so excited his first time out that he forgets to wait for the signal, and he rushes forth, ejaculating wildly and exposing every member of his party. *'Hoka he,'* he cries. 'It's a good day to die.'"

Victor realized that when he smiled, the boy saw only a show of teeth, which had to be the reason the boy didn't appear to be amused.

"And one who is heading up the charge is thinking, 'You've got that right, you dickhead.'" His eyes were beginning to water, and his shoulders shook from suppressed laughter. "'We're in for it now.' And they plunge into the abyss head-on, full steam ahead." He slid one palm across the other in a taking-off gesture as he dissolved into an unseemly fit of choked-off giggles.

"I'm sorry." It took considerable effort, but he pulled himself together. "When I get going, sometimes I just can't stop myself. You probably don't get it, and that's just as well." Another pat on the knee. "Just as well. The bottom line is simply that we must not cry out and give away our position. That would spoil our mission. Our missionary position." Another grin. "I could have been a comedian."

"Instead of a kidnapper?" Victory chided in his ear. "Either way, you were destined to behave like a fool. But so be it. You have rescued the treasures of our people."

"Yes, I have." He turned to the boy. "With your unwilling assistance, I have completed an important mission. You see? You have already been a great help to me. Perhaps you can find some comfort in knowing that you . . .

"I hate seeing such anxiety in your eyes, little brother." He could suddenly smell the boy's fear. He dipped his hand into the deep pocket of his long tunic. "I have medicine. I can share it with you. I can make all your worries go away."

The pocket produced a plastic bag rather than the proper leather bundle, which would not have inspired fear when the boy saw it.

"You're still a child," Victor said quietly. "You're afraid of the needle."

The boy shook his head, nodded, shook his head again.

"Don't look at me like I'm a monster. I'm not a monster. Will you stop looking at me that way?"

The boy closed his eyes and nodded vigorously.

"All right. That's good." Victor put the medicine away. "I'll tell you a story about a young warrior's first mission. Do you like stories, little brother?"

The boy nodded.

"I know you do. You know me from the stories. You know that Victor has no real allies, no friends." Victor patted the boy's leg. If he wasn't mistaken, the trembling had abated. "Until now."

chapter 13

IF WAITING FOR WORD OF AARON WAS BAD, getting the word from Cassandra was worse. Not that she knew any more than Tom did, but the word she was dancing around was *suspect,* and he was her main man. He told himself to let it go, let her go, let it *all* go and lose himself in the work. He took a shot at it, but it was no go.

Okay, maybe he didn't have to lose himself completely. Given free rein, maybe these high-flying emotions of his could actually improve the work. Take a hint from Jesse Brown Wolf and make the anger and the pain work for you. Put a runaway kid into the story. No, a *kidnapping.* Deal with it on paper. Few crimes were more dreadful, more terrifying. *Some sleeze meets a kid on the Internet and lures him into a trap.*

Tom buried his face in his hands. How was it possible to deal with such a thing on paper or anywhere else? If he'd read about the incident in the newspaper, no problem. He could take those vicarious fears and translate them directly into his story. But his fears were attached to a real kid. Whenever he closed his eyes, he saw Aaron's face. Whenever he put pencil to paper, he drew Aaron's face.

In his mind's eye he could see the boy. He was bound, gagged, and locked in a dark place. Not an outdoor hole, but inside an old building. Tom took a deep breath and nearly choked on fantasy dust. It was a far cry from fairy dust. The kind of dust he smelled was the accumulation of decades of abandonment. In a place once vital, dust carried the taste of loneliness and despair. The nose of a healthy boy rejected it.

The nose of an unhealthy man did not. He was accustomed to the dust, to the loneliness and the despair.

Tom lifted his head in wonder. Did he actually have some feeling for both of the specters he'd conjured? One of them was a kidnapper, for God's sake.

His hand trembled as he put his pencil to work, but too soon the clear-born image grew cloudy.

Tom tossed the pencil across the desk. He had sketched a boy's face, the back of another head, and a bunch of boxes. The boxes were filler. When he couldn't think of anything else, he always drew circles or boxes.

He was about to look for something to eat when he thought he heard a knock at the door. More mind games, he thought, but when he heard the sound again, he knew it had to be Angela. Even so, he wished for Aaron. Angela would have to be reminded of his rules for visitors. Aaron would be a miracle.

It was the next best thing to a miracle.

The foolish heart that didn't care what she thought of him thumped wildly at the sight of Cassandra's face. Stepping back to let her in, Tom was forced to bury his hands in the pockets of his jeans to keep his arms from reaching for her.

"Any word?" he asked gruffly.

"No, there's none." As she spoke she closed the door by stepping back against it, hands behind her.

He wondered whether they were both beating down the same urge.

"I came because I don't know what else to do." She shrugged off her coat. "I went to see your mother and managed to offend her completely. I guess I might as well finish the job."

"Do you want something to drink first, or would you rather just have at it?"

She stared at him and bit her lower lip, not in a coy way, but in accord with her claim that she was at a loss, even for an answer to a simple offer.

"You need a drink first." He took her coat and laid it over the back of a chair. "And I'll need a double," he decided as he plunked a bottle of brandy on the counter. "This is the hardest stuff we carry, ma'am."

"That's fine."

He poured, handed her a snifter, and felt her slip away from him as he poured a glass for himself. With the touch of a few buttons, he turned lights off and retracted huge drapes, opening the apartment up to city lights. He watched Cassandra drift toward a window, her fluid, silky dress caressing her willowy body with the light touch his hands would give her if he put them within reach of her.

"You said you wanted to do a job on me," he reminded her from a distance. "Is there any hope that I might enjoy it?" He begged her indulgence with a quick gesture as he approached. "Before you answer, let me add that it wouldn't take much, as long as it's you doing . . ."

She started to turn, and the profile of her face, silhouetted against the window, took his breath away. He finished in a whisper, ". . . almost anything you want to me. As long as it's you."

"Oh, Thomas, I wanted so much to give you those drawings."

"I don't want to hear any more about those drawings, Cassandra. Whoever took them, I hope it's somebody who knows where they belong."

"You would know. You would put them in the proper place."

"Damn right I would. But the way I see it, they've served their purpose in my life. They brought us together, for whatever that's worth." He turned to watch the city lights shimmer in the river. "Now they're off to someplace else. All those horses, all those buffalo, all the hunters and dancers, maybe they've run off to Indian country."

"Do you think so?" Cassandra's gaze followed the direction of Tom's. She wrapped her arms around her slight body, as if she felt a chill. "Do you think Aaron could be with them?"

Her suspicion cut him to the core, but the desolate tone in her voice rendered him defenseless. Unable to comfort or touch or change what was, he suffered in stinging silence.

"I would do anything to get him back safely, Thomas," she said finally. "I don't know what he has to do with the theft of those drawings. I've thought about it and thought about it, and the only thing that makes sense is that he was the means to an end."

"You're right. When you put it all together, that is the only answer that makes any sense."

"I went to the school today, hoping I could get some forgotten clue from one of the kids or from Angela. No one knows him like we do, Thomas. He has no friends except us."

Thomas acknowledged the sad truth with a sigh.

"He would follow you anywhere."

"I rarely *go* anywhere," he said quietly, stepping closer.

"Is it possible that he stumbled onto something, got in the way of something? Some plan, some . . ." With an ostensibly inadvertent gesture, she forestalled his imminent touch. "Thomas, I'm certain someone has been prowling around my house."

"Aaron knew where the drawings were. You said I could show them to him. Remember?"

"Did you happen to mention that to anyone else? That he had—"

"That he had a key to your house and access to the drawings? No!" He backed away, drained his glass, lowered his voice. "No, I didn't tell anyone. Who would I tell? I have less daily contact with people than Aaron does." He turned to put his glass down. "But I had some ledger drawings liberated from a collector in one of my stories. Is that what you're driving at?"

"No. I haven't seen that one."

"What? You don't read my stuff? Actually, it hasn't come out yet. Coming soon to a bookstore near . . ." His quick, hard laugh ended in a groan. "That story had nothing to do with the White Bull drawings. I turned the story in long before I heard about them going up for auction. And when I saw them in the auction catalog, I thought if I could get them, I'd give them to the college on my reservation. But there was no way you were going to let me have them at any price."

"Not then," she said quietly. "I would now."

"Now neither one of us has them. They ran away." Again he turned to the window. His mind eddied around the drawings and then drifted back to the sketch he'd made earlier. "Sometimes I get so deep into the work that I actually see it happening."

"You have a wonderful imagination."

"No, I know the difference. I know when I'm using my imagination, and when it seems to be using me."

"What do you mean?"

"Sometimes I make something up, and it actually happens. Before it's published." He glanced to see whether she was laughing at him yet. Since she was in no laughing mood, he confided, "Truth is, it creeps me out sometimes."

"Strange coincidences can be very creepy."

"Then that's what we have here. A string of creepy coincidences." He sighed. "And a missing boy."

"Who knew where the drawings were," she added. "And now the drawings are also missing."

"And you've come here looking for them. Look around, Cassandra. Where would I hide them?" He strode to one of two eight-foot urban-scape paintings that appeared to hang on the brick wall. "Over here? This is a closet." At his touch, the painting swung open to reveal a small, dark room. "Slick, huh? The doors blend right into the wall. Come on over here and take a look."

Staring in wonder, she stood her ground between the sofa and the window.

"Are you afraid of my skeletons, Cassandra?"

"No."

"Afraid I'll lock you in?"

"No. I don't think you'd—"

"That wouldn't make much sense, would it? Who would pay the ransom, or whatever it is I'm after?"

"I'm only searching for some hint, some trace of my nephew. Darcy's at home now, waiting by the phone, and I can't just sit around," she said, approaching him as she spoke.

He turned on the closet light, revealing shelving and shoes, hanging clothes, in-line skates, the snowshoes he meant to try out the next time he went up north.

She took a glance, but she was more interested in him, a close-up look at his face, into his eyes. He had to wonder what she saw, or thought she saw.

"I'm sorry, Thomas. I can't rule out the possibility that you or someone you know . . ."

He turned out the light and closed the closet door. He had possibilities in mind, too, and there was only one way to rule on them.

"Because, you see, we all came together at the intersection of those drawings," she chattered in the dark.

"I see your point." He also saw that she didn't put her arms around him when he embraced her, but neither did she resist. "And what do you see, Cassandra?" He kissed her before she could say anything he didn't want to hear.

"Do you want to rule this out?" Again, he took a kiss from her for an answer. "Do I scare you?" he whispered.

"No."

He swept her up in his arms and carried her several steps to the sofa. "If I'm a thief and a kidnapper, why aren't you afraid of me?"

"I don't know."

"Yes, you do. You know all, Cassandra. You . . ." He leaned over the back of the sofa and laid her down on the seat. ". . . see . . ." His body followed hers, his knees bracketing her hips. ". . . all. Am I scaring you, Cassandra?" he asked as he took off his shirt.

She shook her head slowly, mesmerized. She reached up, ran a cool palm over his chest. Her lips formed a word, but with her face in the shadows, he couldn't read it. Unless he heard differently, the word would be all he wanted it to be—an affirmation, a compliment, a come-on.

Bring it on, baby.

Jesus, she was killing him just by touching his tits. He undid the buttons on the front of her dress, neck to hem, and unhooked her bra. Her soft breasts spilled into his hands. He buried his face between them and took his turn worrying her nipples with his thumbs, making them hard, giving each one a good tongue-lashing, keeping it up until she moaned so sweetly that he could hardly stand to be separate from her in any way.

"Tell me why you're not afraid of me," he whispered hotly.

"I refuse to be. I don't want to give you up."

"I'm not yours to give up, any more than you're mine

for the taking." He pushed himself up, slid his hand between them, and made a teasing foray over her silky panties. "Are you?" The dampness between her legs heated him to melting inside, tempered him to such hardness on the outside that he knew he would soon crack. "Are you, Cassandra?" he demanded.

"I am," she whispered, "yours for the taking."

He slipped his fingers into her panties and drove her to shivering madness with thumb and middle finger, then with tongue, then, finally, with crowing cock, and the incoming, becoming one, coming as one, oh, oh, oh the thrill was without equal.

He loved watching her sleep in the hours that followed. It was like holding moonlight in his arms, and he couldn't bear the thought that daylight would take her from him.

"I don't want you to give me up, Cassandra," he whispered near her sleeping ear. "Don't ever give me up."

CASSANDRA COULDN'T REMEMBER THE last time she'd felt so good she wanted to cry and so guilty that she just might. She hardly knew her own mind anymore, and her heart had turned certifiably radical. How could she have spent the night with Thomas when Aaron was missing? Why would she make love with him, and how dare she enjoy it? It was such inappropriate behavior, so unlike her. And the next thought—the one she wanted to rip from her head and smash on Darcy's driveway—was that it was something her sister would do.

Cassandra parked her car and went looking for the castigation she deserved.

But it wasn't going to come from Darcy, who wasn't afraid to let her neediness show. "You weren't home last night, Cassie," she said in a voice so reedy that it drew Cassandra to put her arms around her immediately.

"I had my cell phone on all night," Cassandra said, knowing how lame it sounded. "You don't look like you slept at all. You should have called me."

"I drove over to your house." Darcy slid away, offering an apologetic glance. "I know. I was supposed to stay home. I wasn't gone long."

Cassandra felt sick. Her sister looked worried and worn, and she was apologizing for seeking comfort. Her throat burned, and she knew that whatever she tried to say now would make her cry, which she had no right to do. She reached for Darcy's hand and squeezed it hard.

"I've got caffeine shakes," Darcy told her with a little laugh. "Can you tell?"

Cassandra nodded.

"Were you with him? The artist known as Thomas Warrior?"

"I had my cell phone on all night," Cassandra repeated in a husky, teary voice.

"Oh, Cassie." Darcy took her smaller, older, occasionally wiser but never more affectionate sister in her arms. "There's no right and wrong here. There's only us, trying to hold each other up."

"And me not doing my share." Cassandra leaned away, embarrassed, uncomfortable, at a complete loss. "I want to go out and look for him, but I can't think of anywhere else to go. I was hoping Thomas . . ." She shook her head and swiped at her tears with her hand. "Stupid, stupid, stupid."

"Him?"

"Me!" Cassandra spouted. "This whole thing, it's all too crazy. Why can't we just wake up from this nightmare and have everything back the way it was before that stupid auction?"

"My sensible, self-possessed sister," Darcy said as she walked Cassandra to the sofa and sat them both down. "What's he really like? I'm betting on total stud, but looks can be deceiving."

Cassandra snatched a tissue from the box on the side table.

"I hated it when you married Edgar," Darcy told her.

"Why?"

"Because he completed your design for total security. You had everything you wanted—education, fortune, house, husband, and father—and you left me to fend for myself with Mom."

"I offered to pay for you to go to school, but you weren't interested."

"How do you know what I was interested in?"

Cassandra looked at her sister, astonished.

"I'm sorry, but how did you know, Cassie?"

"I guess because you didn't accept my offer."

"But how do you know I wasn't interested?" Darcy touched her sister's knee. "Believe it or not, taking money from my sister isn't a whole lot of fun." She offered an apologetic smile. "Asking for it is even less fun, but guess what? You can void that last check. I didn't need it after all."

"Use it for Aaron," Cassandra urged. "Or yourself. Do something with it for yourself. If you're interested in taking some classes, go for it, Darce."

"I didn't say I was interested. I don't think I ever said anything either way. You're the one who wanted me to go to school."

"I wanted to give you the opportunity," Cassandra said quietly.

"As always, trying to do the right thing. The right things don't work out for me the way they do for you. I know, I know—you *make* things happen, the right things, the right way." She shrugged. "I *let* things happen. Maybe it's not the best way to be, but it's my way to be."

Cassandra nodded, again squeezing Darcy's hand. It was probably a good thing she was too choked up to do much talking. A perfectly levelheaded if cold response was undoubtedly drowning on the tip of her tongue.

"Why is this so hard for us?" Darcy wondered.

"It's me." Cassandra's nod became a headshake. "I've never been very touchy-feely. You know that."

"When you were sixteen and you got to start dating, I'd go to bed, but I'd fight to keep my eyes open, watching the clock for curfew hour to roll around," Darcy recalled.

"I was always on time, wasn't I?"

"You were a very good girl, Cassie." Darcy laughed, remembering gently. "You'd tell me where you went and who you saw and what you did. I'd say, 'What's Johnny really like?' and you'd tell me things he said, word for word. You'd tell me how many times you let him kiss you and how it felt. You don't remember, do you?"

"I do remember." Cassandra gave a misty smile. "I got after you for being awake, but if you'd fallen asleep, I probably made a little extra noise getting ready for bed. It's important to tell those stories right away, while your heart's still pounding like crazy."

"Then tell me now. What's he like? Besides young and studly."

"Definitely studly, but he doesn't seem that young." She leaned back, laying her head against the sofa, side by side with her sister. "Suddenly I don't feel that old. I think we meet somewhere in the middle, Thomas and I."

"What happens in the middle? Is Cassie, at long last, touchy-feely?" Darcy elbowed her. "Lovey-dovey, maybe?"

"Maybe." Cassandra gave a sidelong glance. "But that's not why I went to his apartment last night. I went over there for the same reason I went to the school yesterday afternoon."

"Oh, come on, Cassie. Give me a break." Darcy sat up with a sigh. "While you're at it, give yourself a break."

"But I'm sure there's something we're missing. Aaron must have said something to *someone* somewhere along the line that would point us in his direction. One thing I learned at the school was that when he told me he didn't really have any friends at school, he wasn't just being a mopey kid. He's practically invisible with the kids at school."

"He won't do anything most kids like to do," Darcy

grumbled. "I've told him, you know? Touch football—he could be a linebacker or whatever those big guys play—basketball, rollerblading. Paintball—you know, use the paint to play guns and get all messy, like most kids love to do. But not Aaron."

"What really bothers me is that we didn't see it for what it was before this happened."

"What do you mean, *we?* I knew he didn't have any friends. Marbles—he could play marbles. It doesn't have to be a physical sport. It could be chess, Old Maid, something that takes more than one person." Darcy sighed. "But you're always talking up his artistic talent, Cassie. You've turned him into a one-man show. And he's already getting fat, for God's sake. Twelve years old, and he's a little tub."

"That won't help him, Darce. You can't—"

"I know I can't!" Darcy pounded her forehead with the heels of her hands. "But sometimes I do. Oh, God, it's so frustrating. Sometimes I wonder where he came from. He certainly doesn't take after me." She quickly glanced at her sister. "And you're thinking, 'Thank God.'"

"I'm thinking that I haven't been lovey-dovey enough with either one of you. He's talented and sweet and lonely and very, very vulnerable."

"You don't believe he ran away," Darcy said quietly.

"I think he would be back by now if he'd run away."

"Oh, my God, Cassie, I can't think about the alternatives." Darcy buried her face against Cassandra's shoulder, and they held each other.

"Oh, God, please, *please . . .*"

"Don't let anyone hurt him," Cassandra whispered.

chapter 14

JESSE'S DESK WAS A THROWBACK TO another time. He could hear keyboards clicking from desk to desk throughout the station, but as long as he had a full pencil cup, no computer would be gathering dust in his space. Not that he didn't deal with his share of computer-generated papers, like the fistful Murphy had just handed him. He stared at the first e-mail message from "Victor" to Aaron Farmer.

Don't tell our mutual friend.

It sounded like something straight out of a movie. He could just see some mad, wild-eyed fiend flickering his tongue, slavering over a boy who looked to him like a big dumpling. A couple of messages down the line, the boy had agreed to meet his cartoon hero in a city park Jesse knew well. He had lived there in the days of his own madness.

Whoever this Victor really was, he had read Tom's stories. It might have been someone Tom knew personally. Or not. Jesse didn't see anything in Victor's notes that couldn't have been taken directly from the comic books.

From all accounts, Aaron was a bright kid. Why would he go for this ploy? Why wouldn't he show the Victor messages to Tom, whom he obviously trusted completely? Tom had already warned him about computer crackpots. One of the messages instructed him to delete all their correspondence, which he had only done in the incoming mail file. Clearly neither Victor nor the boy knew much about computers.

Tom's computer would be next. Nobody in the department had said anything about it to Jesse, but he knew the drill. There was suddenly a deafening silence around him at the precinct, which meant that his son was a prime suspect. Nothing pulled down more sympathy for a fellow cop than busting his kid. But it was a quiet kind of sympathy. Jesse welcomed the space officers and staff alike suddenly allowed him by taking the long way around his desk. He needed the space to work through the bizarre course of a case that could be the most important one of his life, even though it wasn't his. It wasn't much of a stretch to figure that the boy's disappearance and the theft of his aunt's ledger drawings were connected somehow. The obvious link was Tom.

Jesse took a drive to the park, where a dozen or more officers were systematically sweeping the grounds for signs of the boy. He left his vehicle down the street and watched the search from a distance. The best nose out there belonged to Magnum, a sharp German shepherd. Jesse had an uncanny way with dogs, and he'd worked with the K-9 corps for a couple of years. He liked the dogs, but he also had a way with kids.

Tom did, too. There was no way he'd had anything to do with any of this. Not knowingly, anyway. But Tom figured into the puzzle somehow, probably the key piece. He had some crazy fans. Angela had told him about some of the weird letters Tom received.

Not that Jesse had any right to judge. He'd been pretty high on the weirdness scale when he'd made his home underground in the nearby river bluffs. He kept an eye on the sweep, but when his fellow officers disappeared from view, Jesse slipped into the bushes.

His well-hidden hole was still there after more than fifteen years. The only visitors he'd had when he'd lived there were Angela and Tommy T. He was sure Angela wouldn't be able to find it anymore. But Tom would. When he was a kid, they'd had a tacit agreement to keep the place a secret, and they'd joke about it being a poor man's lake cabin. Without giving away its location, Tom had used the cave in some of his stories, turning it into an exotic and fascinating underground world beneath the meat-and-potatoes city of Minneapolis.

Who else knew about it?

The entry was overgrown with brush, and there was no sign of human presence. Jesse moved quietly, lowered his body carefully, and stood in near darkness, listening. The scent of deep earth had once given him comfort, but this was no homecoming.

His blood ran cold, filling his head with visions of what he might find in the tunnel as he gripped a small flashlight, which he wouldn't need until he reached the deep room. He'd rather not find himself looking down the barrel of a gun, but he'd much prefer it over discovering a dead child.

At the end of what he'd once thought of as the front hallway, he found nothing but old memories. He flashed his light on the remnants of the place where he'd slept. It was hard to imagine putting himself to bed there now, but his bones remembered the cold, and his hands remembered nursing Angela there after she'd been attacked in the street. The shelves he'd made had become a pile of twigs. He examined the residue on a flat rock and determined it to be wax from a candle he'd burned a lifetime ago.

No one had been there in fifteen years. If anyone could be certain of that, it was Jesse Brown Wolf. At once beset by relief, disappointment, and the threat of the worst headache he'd had in years, he leaned against the earthen wall and injected himself with the drug he'd been prescribed to ward off the pain.

IT HAD BEEN SOME TIME SINCE TOM HAD stopped in at schhool to see Angela, just to talk. After he'd left home, her classroom had become his favorite place to hook up with her. He'd always liked school, but never more than when he'd been living on the streets. School was a safe haven, a place where he could be a kid for a while. Angela had changed that for him by giving him a home.

He peeked into her classroom and smiled to see her working at her desk. He knew what would happen as soon as he made a sound, and part of him hated to do it, but part of him couldn't resist. His deep, soft "Hey!" made her throw up her hands and shriek as though he'd just popped his head through the wall.

It felt good to laugh.

"Tommy, don't you do that anymore!" Her hand flew

to her chest. "Oh, my God. Tommy!"

"What?" He pushed off the doorjamb. "Angela?"

She waited until he'd nearly jumped over the desk before she smiled and wagged her finger at him. "Gotcha."

"I'll be damned," he muttered, catching himself on the front edge of the big desk with both hands, head drooping between his shoulders. He lifted his face slowly, grinning. "Fair warning. I owe you."

"Actually, you've had that coming for years. But one day you will give me a heart attack, sneaking up on me like that."

"I wasn't even trying." He sat on the small desk directly in front of hers. "You're a pathetically easy target for an accomplished sneak."

Her smile fell away. "Any news?"

He shook his head. "Has Jesse told you anything he might not want to tell me?"

"He said you went to see him, which I was glad to hear. I wish it could have been for a different reason." She looked at him sadly. "The chances of finding him alive diminish dreadfully as the hours pass."

"Did Jesse say that?"

"We all know that, don't we? Nobody wants to say it or even think it, but we hear those statistics every time one of these awful stories hits the news." She sighed. "This is the closest I've ever been."

"So let's save the statistics for the next kid."

"I'm sorry, Tommy." She pushed the papers she'd been working on aside. "You were just minding your own business, and I had to find a way to get you involved with—"

"When did you realize that you were in love with Jesse?" he asked. Anyone else would have thought his question had come out of the clear blue, but Angela knew him, knew that he was given to say whatever was on his mind without much preamble.

He could always count on her to answer him the same way.

"Hard to say. I was pretty confused about who he was. There was a time when I thought I might be in love with two individuals—one man and one phantom."

The word *phantom* made Tom smile. "Conflicted, were you?"

"That's an understatement. But when you're a basket case to begin with—which I was, in spades—conflicted seems almost normal." She got that dreamy thinking-about-Jesse look in her eyes. "I loved watching him around kids, especially you. He was so caring and protective. He gave everything he had when he saw kids in need. I loved him for that."

"Is that the way it works? A woman loves a man for certain things he does? Or is it the way he does things? Jesse was always talking about doing things *in a good way*. It was like being raised by Chief Dan George or something. That movie, *Little Big Man*?" Tom chuckled. "We were doing Tommy T Little Warrior becomes Little Big Thomas Warrior."

"With the help of Jesse Brown Wolf and his alter ego, Dark Dog."

"Dark Dog was my creation," Tom protested. "I gave Jesse an identity when he badly needed one."

"You believed in him so passionately, you made him believe in himself."

He hardly remembered what it was like, but he nodded anyway. "I guess he owes me one, huh?"

"You never asked for the things most kids want. Clothes, toys, games, your own car, none of that stuff."

"I was never that kind of kid. I don't know if I was ever any kind of kid."

"You were the kind of kid who believed. You weren't into Santa Claus or clapping your hands red to make Tinkerbell come back to life." She smiled when he rolled his eyes at her. "You were into superheroes."

"A guy can make a good living believing in—"

"A *living,* Tommy, a living, breathing man is only human. You refused to accept Jesse as a human being. You expected him to save everyone you cared about."

"Save? I didn't ask him to save Stony." He braced his hands on his knees. "You think I don't know how bad off my brother was? I almost had him talked into trying rehab again." His hands became a yield sign in response to her dubious look. "Okay. Okay, Stony's a hard case. He's obviously using again. He never comes around me when he's using." Tom scowled. "But Jesse still owes me one, and Aaron's the one he owes me."

"It's not his case, but if I know Jesse, he's keeping close tabs."

"We need more than close tabs. We need his canine nose." He moistened his lips as he shifted gears. "What do you think of Cassandra?"

"I think of her as a friend, or more like an acquaintance, I guess. I don't exactly hobnob in her social circles."

It was his turn to flash the incredulous look.

"What?"

"I don't think she's exactly a hobnobber, Angela."

"She has to be. Doesn't she? I mean, raising money for charities, museums, the arts. Isn't that what those people do?"

He stared at the student paper atop her stack, recognizing the big, round, dark handwriting of someone concentrating on the formation of each letter in each word on the spelling list. Some words were clearly harder to deal with than others.

"You told me once that you were looking forward to the day when I'd come home and say, 'Mom, I think I'm in love,'" he reminded her quietly.

"I remember telling you that my fondest wish for you is—"

"Mom, I think I'm in love."

They stared at each other for a moment. She wasn't squealing and hugging and coming up with names for the children the way he'd imagined she would. She was simply sitting there behind her desk, as though he hadn't come up with a complete answer, but the teacher still had hope for him.

She lowered her gaze to his hands. "She's a good bit older than you are, isn't she?"

"I haven't counted her teeth, but I think they're all there." What was a *good bit,* anyway? It didn't sound like a bad thing, so he chuckled.

She didn't, but he thought he detected the hint of a smile.

"All I know is, I've never felt this way about a woman, not even close." He leaned into his argument. "There are a lot of differences between us that don't matter, but there's one that does." His momentum lost its steam. "I don't think she feels the same way about me."

"Not even close?"

"I don't know." He'd thought about the things she'd said, questions she'd asked about the drawings and Aaron and who knew what about either or both. "Even when you were unsure of Jesse's identity, you knew his heart. You trusted him."

"And Cassandra doesn't trust you," Angela concluded.

"She's playing detective."

"Understandable. We're all racking our brains for details that might help in the search."

"She thinks I stole those ledger drawings."

"Did she say that?"

He sighed. "Like I said, she's playing detective. Why would I take them? She offered to give them to me."

"That's what she said."

"And she thinks I had something to do with Aaron's disappearance."

This was clearly the first thing he'd said that was news to Angela. "She actually accused you of—"

"Don't start sharpening your claws, Mrs. Brown Wolf. It wasn't like a bold-faced accusation." He backed off and shrugged. "Maybe it was. And maybe it looks bad. The cops questioned me. They even took my computer this morning."

"Your computer?"

"I'm the one who told them about Aaron cruising around the Internet looking for information about weird stuff like vampires and cannibals. They probably would have checked out his computer anyway, but, hey, why would I tell them if I had anything incriminating on my own computer? Did they take your computer? Or Cassandra's?"

"They didn't take ours."

"I don't use the thing that much, and I don't have a problem with them looking under every rock. That's what they get paid for. I don't care if they suspect me." His gesticulations stopped on a dime. "I care that *she* suspects me."

"Have you asked her how she feels about you?"

"Hell, no." He raised a warning finger. "Don't you do it, Angela."

"Would I do a thing like that? If you really loved me, you wouldn't point that finger at me, Tommy." Then gently she asked, "Have you told her how you feel?"

"Hell, yeah." He could tell that she knew better. "Not in so many words, but . . ."

"Three isn't so many. You're holding one back, aren't you?"

"Waiting for the right time, and it's for damn sure this ain't it."

"Sometimes people fall in love so hard and so fast, they don't know which way is up. And they don't really know each other. That takes time." She rose from her chair and skirted the desk as she approached him. "Which is why I tried to teach you the importance of taking the time before taking to the sheets."

"Do you mind not going there? I love you, Mom, but I'm thirty years old—"

"Don't rush it." She laid a hand on his shoulder and smiled into his eyes. "See how easy that was to say?"

"Thirty?"

She shook her head.

"I love you," he said quietly.

"Mom," she persisted. "So much easier than Angela."

He slipped one arm around her waist and permitted her to tussle his curly hair without protest.

elsewhere

VICTOR CREPT BAREFOOT DOWN SPIRALING cast-iron steps and burst through the small door to his secret home, longing to slam it behind him. His commitment to silence had its disadvantages at times like this.

Fortunately, his new friend was all eyes and ears for Victor's venting.

He circled behind the chair and bent over the boy's head. "Why would the cops take Thomas's computer?" he demanded. "How would they connect him? Did you erase all our messages like I told you to?"

The boy's head bobbed.

"I did, too. I don't use it much, so I won't miss it. They must be checking up on everybody who knows you, huh?" He leaned around the side of the chair. "You're sure you deleted everything?"

The boy nodded as vigorously as he could manage.

"We don't want them connecting Thomas to our alliance. His ass would be on the line, not ours. He sticks his neck out every time he publishes something with his name on it, you know."

He adjusted his coyote face as he squatted next to the arm of the chair. "I don't have to worry. I'm just a character in a comic book. And you don't have to worry. You're just a kid. But you and me and Victory, we have to protect Thomas." Victor tapped the boy's fettered arm with an easy fist. "Are you with me, little brother?"

Not only did the boy affirm his allegiance, but he also stuck out his chin and wiggled as much of his lips and nose as the sturdy silver tape permitted.

"I can't let you speak yet." Victor gave the boy's arm what he hoped would be taken as a reassuring pat. "You have a ways to go in your training. You must listen long and hard before speaking will be permitted. Do you notice how quietly I am able to move and speak? You'll learn quickly if you don't speak. Only watch and listen.

"You know, you have already provided invaluable help in an important mission." Victor reached into the pocket of his gray tunic and brought out a key. "We have liberated the old drawings from the white woman who held them in her keep. Let me show you."

Victor leaped into the darkness, unable to contain his enthusiasm for showing someone the proof of his cunning. He scurried back to the chair, into the small circle of light that surrounded it, where he presented his plunder with pride.

"Securing these treasures is our victory," he declared as he displayed the familiar drawings one by one. "Once the commotion dies down, Thomas will deliver them into the proper hands, and he will tell the people that we served them well in this." He looked up from the floor into wide, attentive eyes. "I realize that this woman is closely related to you, but the mission always comes first. Would you like to be adopted into the tribe?" The boy made no move as he stared at the drawings. "Thomas can arrange that for you."

The boy flashed Victor a fearful look.

"What? You need the can? You want food?" Carefully stowing the artwork in its case, he muttered, "I'll hunt up some food."

He returned from the darkness with pieces of his favorite pink meat piled on the sharp-edged aluminum lid of a five-pound coffee can.

"We'll share." He helped himself to the first bite. "You know what this is, don't you?"

The boy shook his head.

"This," he said, pointing to the jagged plate, "was taken from your chamber pot. No one will nag you to put the lid down, you see, because we have found a real use for it. And this . . ." He couldn't resist helping himself to another bite. "Well, you'll know when you taste it.

"Now, let's see how much you have learned." The boy flinched when the tape was ripped from his cheek just to the corner of his mouth. "You are not to speak while you eat. One word, and your meal is over. The tape goes back on. Do you understand?"

The boy nodded, dubiously eyeing the piece of meat on its journey to the side of his mouth. Victor pulled the tape halfway across his mouth and slipped the food into the slot, slick as mailing a letter.

He laughed at the boy's unmistakable relief. "Good ol' Minnesota Spam." Still chuckling, Victor fed his friend another piece, leaning close to confide, "You learn fast, little brother. Together we will be like Dark Dog and his little Fox."

As Victor offered a second morsel, the boy suddenly bucked in his chair and craned his neck, achieving a butting of heads and nearly biting the hand that fed him.

"What are you doing?" Victor spat.

The threat of an answer was quickly sealed off with tape. Not a word, he had warned, and the boy could not be permitted to defy him.

Victor sat back on the floor, sadly surveying the scattered pieces of food. When he'd lived in the streets, he'd tamed several timid creatures with precious bits of food. It was a thing that required patience.

He stood, assuming his full height over the boy in the chair.

"Had you displaced my face, you would no longer be my ally." He leaned close to the boy's ear. "Please don't make me kill you, little brother."

chapter 15

"WILSON AND KEPPEL JUST BROUGHT YOUR son in, Jess."

Jesse had spent the morning pulling a scared kid away from his dim-witted mother and her abusive boyfriend.

He tossed his blue jacket on top of one exactly like it that shouldn't have been on his peg, and then turned, trying to shift his gears from a preteen turned kicking-and-screaming-*Mama* little boy to Murphy's news.

"My son?"

"Those messages to the Farmer boy must have come from Tom's computer, man. They're on the hard drive."

"Holy shit," Jesse muttered. He had no use for computers, but he'd seen the strange "Victor" messages in plain black and white. There was only one possible explanation. "Somebody's gotta be setting him up. Where is he?"

Stupid question. Jesse grabbed his clipboard off the top of the coatrack and headed for the interrogation room with Murphy in tow. "Maybe it's one of those computer worms they're always talking about. How does that work?"

"I don't know, man." Murphy hurried to catch up. "I couldn't get my bank account balance the other day because of a worm. You talk about your weapons of mass destruction. Jess—" He grabbed Jesse by the arm. "You know you can't do that."

Jesse drew back, slowly releasing the handle of the door he desperately wanted to open. "Did he call his lawyer?"

"I don't know."

The two men slipped quietly into the next room and stood behind the one-way window. Jesse tried to ignore the churning in his gut as he watched Tom calmly answer the questions the two officers put to him. Pete Keppel sat across the table with pad and pencil. He was a big, beefy man whose face always looked almost as red as his thinning hair. Older and more experienced, Steve Wilson was a wiry pacer.

"Help us out with some names, Tom," Keppel coaxed. "Anyone who had access to your apartment and your computer when those e-mails were sent."

"Like I said, I'm not one for entertaining people at home, and I don't keep a calendar. Those dates mean nothing to me."

"How about someone from the school downstairs?"

"They don't have access to my apartment."

"Has Aaron Farmer been in your apartment?" Wilson asked.

"No."

"Have you had any visitors lately?"

"That you know of," Keppel added.

"My mother."

"How about your dad?" Keppel wanted to know.

"He comes under the heading of 'not that I know of.'"

"How far have they gone with this?" Jesse asked Murphy in a barely controlled whisper. "Did they get a search warrant?"

"They asked him nicely, and he gave up the computer without one. He hasn't been charged with anything, but it's more than a fishing expedition. They've got the e-mails."

"He should tell them about some of his freaky fans," Jesse said aside as he watched the proceedings intently.

Murphy elbowed him. "Hey, man, who're you callin' freaky?"

"I'm serious. He's had—"

Tom shot out of his chair. "He's back there, isn't he?" He peered at the window. "Jesse! Come in here and point your damn finger right at my face."

"Your dad isn't—"

Jesse turned on the speaker. "Tom, you need a lawyer. You can put a stop to this right now. Just tell them you won't answer any more—"

"Stop hiding behind the fucking mirror, Jesse." He turned to Wilson. "I want him in here where I can see him."

"If you have an attorney, it might be a good idea for you to call him," Wilson said. "We can continue later."

"I want you guys to find that kid," Tom shouted. "I'll tell you anything you want to know, anything that can help. My mother and the boy's aunt—those are the only two people who've come to my place in weeks. Months."

"Tell them about some of the wackos who write to you about your books," Jesse insisted as he burst through the door of the interrogation room. "Tell them about the ones who want you to write about their friends from outer space, or the guy who said you were going to hell for teaching kids about pagan gods. Or how about that woman who stalked you after she met you at that comic book collectors' convention?"

Tom's heated glare was the same one Jesse had run up against years ago on the day Tommy T had first learned that his hero had been a cop. For a kid who had grown up viewing cops in the same category as monsters and Lakota *gigis*—whatever you do, don't let them get you—accepting a cop as his friend and then as his father was easier said than done.

"That was a long time ago," Tom said quietly as he lowered his gaze.

"It's gotta be somebody like that, Tom. Hell, the asylums are full of people who think they're Superman." Jesse turned to plead his case with Wilson. "Now there's one out there who thinks he's Victor."

"Thinks he's Victor?" Tom echoed, taken aback. "What are you talking about?"

"The guy who contacted Aaron over the Internet called himself Victor and talked about—"

"Would you let us handle this, Jesse?" The warning look in Wilson's eyes clued Jesse in. They hadn't revealed all of the details yet.

"Calls himself *Victor*," Tom echoed incredulously.

"The question is, how did he get access to your computer?" Keppel wanted to know.

Tom turned up an empty palm. "That thing just sits there most of the time. I e-mail my editors, agent, publicity people, do a little shopping sometimes."

"Do you have a website with, like, personal information?"

"The publisher deals with all that stuff. Victor gets mail; I get mail. Victory gets more than either of us." Tom glanced at Jesse. "Not all my readers are wackos. She's a fox."

"In one of the stories, you've got Victor stealing ledger drawings," Jesse said, glancing at Murphy for confirmation.

"Victor's been stealing a bunch of stuff like that," Murphy reminded him. "The ledger drawings were previewed at the end of the last book."

Tom gave an innocent shrug. "He's bringing cultural treasures back to his people. That's the storyline."

"It's more than a storyline. We've had how many of these thefts reported lately?" Keppel asked Murphy.

"Three or four."

"Somebody's obsessed with your stories," Jesse explained to his son. "Some comic book junkie who's gone over the edge."

"How did he get hold of Tom's computer?" Wilson demanded.

"And how did Aaron get messed up in all this?" Keppel added quickly. "Can you help us out with some names? All we've got is Thomas Warrior."

"And Victor," Murphy muttered.

Stoically, Tom shook his head. "I don't know what else to tell you."

"We'll give you some time to think about it," Wilson said as he laid a hand on Tom's shoulder.

"Are you arresting me?"

"We're holding you while we get a warrant to search your place."

"I don't care if you search, but I want to be there." For the first time in years, Tom turned to his father for help. "Jesse, tell them. That's my studio. I've got months worth of work—"

"I'll go along with them. I want you to call your lawyer."

"I don't know who to—" Tom took his keys from the front pocket of his jeans. "Take these. Do you know how to get up there? If they want to check out the two floors I don't use, you'll need this key. But the school . . ."

"It'll be okay, son," Jesse said quietly, his own heart breaking over Tom's obvious willingness to cooperate or hang himself, one of the two.

"I keep thinking how scared Aaron must be. I know what that's like."

Jesse lifted his hand, gave a look, a nod, a chance to refuse. Tom permitted the hand to settle on his shoulder.

They both knew what it was like.

WHILE OFFICERS WILSON AND KEPPEL TOOK Tom to a cell where they would hold him while they searched for enough evidence to charge him with a crime, Jesse called Angela and told her the latest news. She took it quietly.

"I told Tom I'd go along on the search so they can get in without breaking anything. Meanwhile, he needs a good lawyer."

"Can I see him?"

"Not now. Listen, Angela, I've been on the outs with Tom for a long time. I don't know much about what's going on with him, how he works out his ideas, who he—"

"What are you getting at, Jesse?"

"I don't know," he said, giving her a lie with a sigh. She'd been married to a cop long enough to see through it all, at least part way. "None of this makes much sense right now."

"*We* both know that Tom would never hurt that

boy. *Don't we?*"

"Yeah, we do, but who's Victor? Isn't that somebody Tom invented? Somebody's obviously become so obsessed with Tom's fantasy world that he's pretending to be Victor."

"Now, that *does* make sense."

He damn sure hoped so. Leave it at that, he told himself.

But he was already giving voice to the suspicion he'd been trying to fight off.

"Tom's been okay lately, hasn't he? Has he had any medical problems that I don't know about, maybe stress-related, or—"

"You're not suggesting that Tommy has suddenly developed some sort of psychological problem, are you? Because if that's where you're going with this, I can tell you right now, you need to come up with a new theory."

"I don't know where I'm going, Angela." He rested his forehead on the heel of his hand. "I think it's some fan of his. That's what I really think. Anything else is unthinkable."

"Jesse, try to think like a father instead of a cop right now."

"Right now he'll be better served if I think like a cop."

CASSANDRA HAD NO TROUBLE GETTING IN to see Thomas with attorney Carlton Judd pulling the strings. He claimed that they were there to speak to their client, but he dropped Cassandra off at the visitation window and told her that he would be along after he checked to see what the score was. She had relinquished her purse, passed though a metal detector, settled into the chair she was offered, and waited, mentally trying to remove herself from her surroundings.

But when Thomas appeared behind the Plexiglas window, she saw nothing but him and the words she could only read on his lips.

What are you doing here?

She picked up the phone. "Angela called me. She said you needed an excellent lawyer, and I brought you one."

From the look in his dark eyes, he might have been staring through the window at a stranger.

Finally he picked up the receiver on his side. "That's very generous of you." His eyes finally betrayed his sadness. "Get out of here, Cassandra. Please."

"He's the best there is, Thomas. Is there anything else I can do?"

"You should be with your sister. The two of you need to stick together for Aaron's sake. Be there for him when he gets home."

"He'll want to see you, too."

"I'm about to be charged with his kidnapping."

"W-why?"

"Because Victor got into my computer somehow." He wagged his head, half smiling. "Damn crafty, that one. Victory's been saying it all along: you never know what a trickster's gonna do next."

"What are you talking about?"

"Remember when I told you that sometimes my stories seem to come true in some way?"

"And how it creeps you out?"

"Did you think I was crazy when I said that? Was that your first clue?"

"You're going to hate hearing this, but I thought it was cute. Something Indiana Jones might say." She leaned closer to the window, offering what she hoped was an encouraging word. "You didn't do a story about a kidnapping."

"How did Victor get into my computer?"

"Thomas," she scolded softly, "now you're scaring me."

"Yeah, me, too."

"I don't believe in Victor. I believe in you, Thomas. You're a warrior of the heart, and you've conquered mine."

He laughed. Not long, and not hard, but music. Sweet music.

"You talk about cute and scary both, that's a hell of a line, woman." He pressed his palm against the window. "I can't imagine anybody but you saying it and still hanging on to her dignity."

"Maybe we're both a little strange," she said softly, matching her hand to his. "I don't mind. But since we both know you didn't kidnap Aaron, we need to get you out of here. Are you ready to meet the best criminal defense attorney in the state?"

"I love a woman with good connections."

"That would be me."

JESSE WATCHED HIS FELLOW OFFICERS search his son's apartment. He couldn't help feeling a sense of pride. The place was classy. Tom's success showed in each refurbished architectural detail and every piece of furniture.

Murphy was impressed, if no one else was. He was more than pleased to help Jesse stand guard over Tom's drawing board. "Just look at this," he enthused over a dark ally scene between Victory and her man-dog counterpart. "The original artwork, man. The colors make some parts of it jump right out at you."

"Some comic book artists use colorists to fill in their drawings, but Tom does his own. He says the color is as important as the words when you're telling a story."

"Great place he's got here. Hey, Kep, show some respect. Put the furniture back the way it was," Murphy ordered, a subtle reminder that he outranked Keppel.

Had the big man's glance been a knife, it would have sliced Murphy ear to ear. "Where does he keep his clothes?" Keppel asked Jesse.

"Drawers are under the bed here," Wilson reported. He was already rifling through the first one.

"Kids, huh? They never learn to pick up their underwear." Murphy winked at Jesse, who was not amused. "Boxers or briefs?" Murphy asked Wilson.

"Box*es*, Murphy. Boxes on casters, as in *drawers,* containing the usual." The older officer flashed a foil packet. "He's practicing safe sex, Dad."

"Give it up, Wilson."

"There must be a closet somewhere," Keppel said.

Wilson closed the drawer he'd been working through and opened the doors on a tall wardrobe. "There's stuff hanging in here," he announced as he flicked crisp shirts on dry-cleaner hangers one by one across the rod. "Nice threads."

"Any female underwear?" Keppel asked as he pulled his head out of a kitchen cupboard.

"Looks to me like he's one of us," Murphy observed.

Wilson laughed. "Except he keeps his place a lot neater than you do."

"Let's have a look downstairs," Keppel said.

"Nice place," Murphy commented as the three men filed past Jesse on their way to the freight elevator. "From the outside, you'd never guess."

"That's the point." Jesse closed the gate on the elevator. "I'm sure nobody bothered him here until now."

The floor below the apartment was dim and dingy with its blackout-painted windows, lack of electricity, piles of crates, and jumble of junk. Jesse played a flashlight beam over the scene.

"This stuff was here when he bought the building. There's two floors like this. How much time have you got?"

Wilson raised his voice to the rafters. "Anyone here? We're police officers. We're looking for Aaron Farmer. It's safe to come out." He clicked on a flashlight and aimed it across the wood floor. "Anyone here? Any sound you can make, we'll find you, son."

"What I don't want to hear is anything scurrying

around the floor," Murphy said. "Or flapping its wings."

"Can't smell anything but dust." Keppel punctuated his observation with a cough. "God, I hate places like this. With all his money, why doesn't he do something with this?"

"What for? He uses places like this in his stories. This is what you call urban gothic."

"Murphy," Jesse mocked, "you don't know what the hell you're talkin' about. *Urban gothic,* for crissake."

"Look at these old windows, Dog." Murphy had discovered a cache of tall stained glass standing against a brick wall.

"They were upstairs. He wanted clear glass."

"See, this is what I mean. What you have here, this is all part of the mood you find in a Thomas Warrior story." Murphy turned his flashlight on the discarded windows and their multicolored pattern of glass blocks. "This stuff is worth some cash. He could get one of those salvage outfits to come in here and—"

Keppel sneezed. "You guys can hang around and discuss this junk collection, but I'm developing an allergy." Three more sneezes proved his claim.

"There's nothing here," Wilson agreed.

Jesse brought up the rear. He was as eager to find the boy as anyone, but not in Tom's building. Please God, he added, and then mentally admonished himself for permitting as much as a prayer.

His boot heel slipped on something. He stopped, squatted on his heels, and furtively scraped it up with the edge of a business card, which he carefully folded and stuffed.

He hoped he was carrying a pocketful of pure, simple rodent shit.

chapter 16

TOM DISCOVERED HOW USEFUL GOOD legal representation could be, even to an innocent man, when he was told he was free to go "for now." He called for a cab, gave the driver his direction—from jail to Lake of the Isles—and ignored the smirk on the man's face as he climbed into the back seat.

He hadn't taken the time to call ahead, but he had a powerful feeling that she was waiting for him. It had been more than twenty-four hours since he'd had anything to eat, and he was fairly sure his apartment had been turned upside down, but there was only one place he wanted to be, one face he needed to see, and both belonged to Cassandra.

He slid down, rested his head against the back of the seat, and closed his eyes. It pleased him simply to roll her name round and round inside his head, draw out the *s*'s and *a*'s so that he felt their reverberation. Cassandra, the fine. Cassandra, the chic. Cassandra, the discriminating. Cassandra, the woman in a sea of girls. Cassandra, the one who believed in him.

Generosity grew with Tom's reverie. With a liberal tip in hand, the cynical driver was more than willing to wait another moment. Disappointment for Tom would clearly be to his benefit.

But Cassandra was also the woman waiting.

"I'm glad you're home," he told her when she came to the door. Without taking his eyes off her, he waved the cab away.

"I'm glad you're here." She took his hands and drew him across the threshold, into her arms. "I'm so glad you're here."

She held him hard and took his hungry kiss into her warm, wet, welcoming mouth. Pure bliss. He longed to follow his tongue, go down inside and live as part of her, safe and warm and deeply cherished.

"I'm sure I'm being watched," he whispered into her hair, and then spoke aloud, a second thought. "Hell, *I'd* watch me if I thought I would lead me to Aaron."

"Isn't that what they call chasing your tail?"

"Are you worried about how it looks, my coming to you?"

She looked up at him with sympathy in her smile and sadness in her eyes. "How it looks to who?"

"Anybody trying to put all these crazy pieces together. I don't want them to start in on you."

"I don't want them to waste time following the wrong man."

"I'm all they've got," he said with a sigh. "Baby, if I don't get something to eat pretty soon, I'm gonna waste away."

"I can't believe I'm letting a man call me 'baby,'" she muttered as she led the way to the kitchen. "Shall I cook you a hot meal, or would you rather have sandwiches?"

"I'm not just any man; I'm your man. And you should cook me a hot sandwich."

She pulled a hearty meal together in short order. Instant mashed potatoes and leftover beef had never tasted so good to him. They sat across from each other in the breakfast nook. She nibbled on a sandwich. He was on his third helping when she replenished the strong black coffee he'd craved.

"The whole time they were grilling me," he told her, "I kept thinking, who's out looking for Aaron while these guys are dickin' around with me? But after a while, you start to wonder. I know I didn't do this thing, but I see why they think I did. I'd probably go there, too. Hell, I know I would; I'd come up with the same answers. They've got answers that make my answers sound shifty. You try to come up with something that makes some sense to them, but ultimately it doesn't make much sense to you.

"Then you feel like you've gone dry, and you're starting to crack. Pretty soon you figure you'll be all over the table, all your little pieces for them to pick through. If it would bring Aaron back, you know, have at it. But I don't know where he is. I swear to God, I'm wracking my brain every waking minute, and I don't have a clue."

Winding down, he set his cup down slowly, targeting a flower on the place mat and speaking softly. "So I came to ask you to help me put the pieces back together."

"I'll do whatever I can."

He covered her hand with his, caressed the softer side of her wrist. "Love me tonight."

"Where would you like me to start? Which pieces?"

"Just love them all. Make them fit together and form a whole man."

She took his plea to heart and took him to her bed, where she took his body to hers. He was hers now as he had never been before—Thomas Warrior, the most beautiful man she had ever known—truly hers for the taking, which she did with profound care.

She thrilled to the touch of his hands and the feel of his mouth, and she touched and tasted in return—the hard rock candy of him, the tang and the salt of him, the musky scent of him, the unflinching devouring of him, even as he—how was it possible?—consumed her.

He made her feel beautiful. He convinced her that the woman he saw when he looked and touched and tasted might begin to approach the beauty she knew in him. He filled her empty places with hot flesh and rushing blood, showed her passion instead of projects and propriety. She welcomed the pleasure of losing herself in him, wrapping herself in him and around him, so that he would never again be truly without her no matter what kind of reality the cold light of day might bring.

Their loving left them languid and slick, awash in each other. Dreading the sleep that would take him from Cassandra to a dark world of his mind's making, he went to the bathroom, filled the tub, and then lured her into the water with the promise of sharing it with her.

She came bearing spicy red wine and herb-scented bath salts. They eased into the hot water, face to face, thighs on thighs, teasing each other with the chance that he might slip inside her again by putting the means agonizingly close to the approach. And they shared cares of all kinds. He loved her softness, and she loved the way the rich color of his skin made the pallor of hers seem pearly. He loved her pink nipples. She loved his sweet, chocolaty eyes.

"But don't you wish they could see in the dark, Cassandra?"

"Your eyes?"

"My eyes," he echoed, lifting his hand from the water, fingers splayed and dripping. "I get the feeling that I've been turning a blind eye to something that looms right here in front of my face."

"Something to do with Aaron?"

"Jesse thinks it's some crazy reader. Sometimes they want me to do stories about certain things, their stuff. Girl gangs, gay sumo wrestlers, George Armstrong Custer's great-great-grandson. I don't know where people come up with this crap, don't care, don't save their letters. But now I'm ripping my brain apart, trying to remember somebody asking me to do a kidnapping."

"Do people confide their fantasies or confess their darkest secrets?"

"I get all kinds of letters from all kinds of places, from Hollywood to homeless shelters. Even prisons." He scooped a handful of water and watched it run through his fingers. "Even prisons," he repeated softly as the water trickled over Cassandra's knee. "I keep thinking about Victor, about who he is and what his traditional purpose is. The Trickster. The antihero. The part of ourselves that trips us up. But without him, God would probably be bored with us, you know what I'm saying? You talk about fully human and fully divine; Victor's that fully human part.

"What I do know is that if you and Aaron hadn't gotten involved with me, he'd be—"

"No, now you're thinking like Victor," Cassandra cautioned. "Victory is much more your style, Thomas."

He smiled. "Victory is a woman."

"So am I. And I'm your style." She took his wet hand and tucked it between her breasts. "So get in touch with the female side. We have no reason to lose hope, Thomas."

"I haven't told you this because I know how crazy it sounds, but I see Aaron alive."

She went still, staring at him as though he'd grown a new head.

"Forget I said that."

She shook her head. "What do you mean, you see him?"

"In my mind," he explained, thinking that if he could get his right leg free without her noticing, he ought to use it to kick himself. "And I'm not claiming to be psychic. When I'm working, sometimes I see things I wasn't thinking about, you know what I'm saying?"

"Not exactly. But that's because I have no imagination. What do you see?"

"I see him in a dark place with his mouth covered, and he's looking up at somebody. That's the part I want to see—the face of the guy he's looking up at. But that part is dark, too. It's like the back of somebody's head. Just enough so I know he's there." He squeezed her hand. "It's nothing, baby. It's so vague, it's only a teaser. Wishful thinking, I guess."

"I think I'm having the same feeling. I don't see any images, but I have a strong feeling that he's alive." Her wistful smile lifted his spirits. "Wishful *feeling?*"

"I tell you what, those ledger drawings haunt me, too," he confided. "Before all this happened, I felt like I was using the energy from those drawings in my work. I'd get in front of a piece of paper with a pencil in my hand, and I'd feel the earth rumble. I'd hear guys shouting at each other, words I didn't know but somehow understood. And I'd smell horse sweat and fresh blood. And I couldn't sketch fast enough."

"And now?"

"It was more energy than image. But since Aaron disappeared, the energy isn't there." He lifted one shoulder. "I haven't done much drawing."

"You haven't had the heart to." She lifted his hand to her lips and brushed them over his knuckles. "I don't know where creativity or creative inspiration comes from, Thomas. But I don't think you're crazy."

"*Going* crazy?"

"If you are, take me with you. I want to go where you go."

"You do, huh?" He drew her bottom along the tracks of his legs. "I want to go inside you again," he whispered at the point of coupling.

Her eyes held his gaze as she put her hands on his shoulders and rose to receive him. "Then I'll take you there."

Their smooth, slick, shivery joining made him groan, made her gasp, made them hold each other still until the exquisite pleasure of coming together had surged in ripples to their extremities, leaving them dry-mouthed and panting. He took her nipple into his mouth like a high port bit, tongued it playfully, making ready to race. She loved the feel of his hot-blooded, edgy prancing, savored it as long as she could handle, then threw her head back and rode him to a place where craziness reigned.

FROM A HILLTOP HE OBSERVED A HERD OF buffalo grazing on new spring grass with their young calves. It should have been a serene sight, but he was restless, and the picture shuddered like an old silent movie, the images shifting form—natural to ledger-likeness, natural, ledger-likeness, jerking back and forth as though White Bull had drawn every other frame.

The view unnerved him, backed him up a step. It was then that he saw the coyote at his feet, watching intently, choosing its prey. One step back had separated the man from the animal. One step. He looked over his shoulder. Behind him was a four-story drop to a city street. One more step back . . .

Tom woke up in a cold sweat, the image of the coyote's profile floating above him. It receded into the bedroom ceiling and vanished before he could see its face. He shot up, desperate to follow.

A cool hand touched his back, and he realized that he was sitting on the side of the bed, trying to get his bearings in the dark.

"Thomas, what is it?"

"Nothing. A dream."

"A bad one?" She scooted up behind him. He felt the imprint of her lovely face on his back. "You're shaking all over."

"If I go over the edge, I'm goin' alone, baby." He drew a tremulous breath and sighed deeply. "It's no place I want to take you."

"Here, let me hold you." She pulled him back into her bed, pressing his face between her breasts. "It was only a dream, Thomas. I'm not letting you go anywhere I can't be."

TOM LEFT HIS WOMAN SLEEPING SWEETLY, as was his custom, but he dreaded going home. He located his spare key in the brick siding and drew a deep breath as he let himself in. His unaccompanied footsteps made for a lonely sound. The echo in the stairwell mocked him for going to such great lengths to seal himself off from the city he loved. He wasn't guarding any national treasures. He was a cartoonist, for God's sake.

He could tell that someone had been searching the place. They hadn't scattered his belongings around, but the wardrobe doors were open slightly, and he could see that the drawers had been pulled out from under the bed. Some clown had left a condom on the nightstand. Tom tossed it back in the drawer. Not Jesse's doing, he told himself. Jesse was a lot of things, but he was no clown. He knew he had Jesse to thank for the fact that he wouldn't be spending the day cleaning up his apartment.

He had stopped at the post office to pick up a pile of mail. He drank orange juice from a quart bottle while he sorted through bills and advertisements, hoping for something to catch his eye, something that was not consistent with his usual mail. He smiled when he turned over a postcard announcing an upcoming auction and read the note from the dealer. *Don't miss this set of ledger drawings. Every bit as significant as the White Bull collection.*

"Yeah, let's go back and start all over," he said aloud. He looked around, as though he actually thought a source of support for the idea might be waiting in the rafters. "What do you think, Victory? Do we want to try for more trouble?"

She wasn't jumping on board. Probably mad at him for ignoring her lately.

So it was literally back to the drawing board. His work wasn't going anywhere without him. No matter what else was going on, he had work to do. Maybe it wasn't a national treasure, but a lot of people enjoyed his stories. If he didn't produce them, they weren't going to happen. Victory's next challenge waited to be discovered at Tom's drawing board.

But another discovery would come first. Six feet from the table, Tom stopped in his tracks. All he could see was a corner of the black leather case, but he knew what lay ahead. More trouble. Sometime after his place was searched, someone had brought him the ledger drawings.

His hands trembled as he pulled the drawings from the case. They were out of order. The drawing on top depicted a herd of buffalo grazing in a prairie draw. On a distant hilltop, a lone coyote watched them.

Tom had seen it all last night, but the dream had

reversed the perspective. He had been on the hill with Coyote.

Who the hell was he?

He picked up the phone and did something he'd never done before these drawings had come into his life. He called a cop.

"Jesse, can you come over to my place?"

"What's goin' on?"

"Somebody left me a gift. Please, just come now. And bring my friend Murphy."

elsewhere

"I'VE TURNED THE TREASURES OVER TO Thomas," Victor told the boy. "I think Victory will be pleased with my decision, don't you?"

There was something to be said for being able to talk to someone he could see, even if they couldn't actually converse with each other.

The boy nodded, his eyes weary but less wary than they had been days ago.

"Am I hearing this right?" said the voice at Victor's back. "You think you've done something that will please me?"

"It's time Thomas took the drawings back where they belong. The police are looking for them now," Victor whispered to the voice in the dark. He glanced at the boy, who didn't appear to be troubled by his discussion with Victory.

"They're looking for the boy, you fool," she said, pulling Victor's attention back to the darkness. "What are you going to do with him?"

"He's my ally. I'm going to keep him."

"There is no ally for one such as you. Haven't you realized that yet?"

"You are my ally, aren't you?" Victor asked his guest.

The boy nodded dutifully.

"Do you hear Victory?"

The boy's head bobbed automatically, like a souvenir nodder with a spring for a neck.

"Did you hear what she called me?"

The nodding stopped as the boy weighed his answer, looking to Victor for a clue.

He laughed. "You can't hear her. That's a privilege you must earn. She speaks only to Thomas and me, but maybe in time she will take you into her confidence."

"Confidence!" Victory's laughter echoed in the dark. "Ah, Victor, you do presume."

Victor moved behind the big overstuffed chair and bent over the boy's head. "She says I have no allies, and Victory is never wrong. I hate that about her. It's good that she knows so much, since I'm not the wisest owl in the woods. But it's hard to live with someone who's never wrong." He petted the boy's fine hair. "So the question goes unanswered. What will I do with you?"

The boy turned his head to the side and tried to look up at him, his eyes expressing the plea he could not voice.

"You're absolutely right. It's only fair to let you have a say." Victor began to peel the silver tape off the boy's cheek. "Let's see how much you've learned about the rules for operating in the netherworld."

The boy clenched his teeth against the sting of tape removal. His eyes teared up but never wavered from the eyes that peered at him through the holes in Victor's coyote face. And he did not speak. He knew better.

"Excellent," Victor whispered. "Now softly, little brother, what do you have to say?"

"I . . . I . . ." Wide-eyed with the wonder of his own stuttering voice, the boy swallowed twice before trying again. "I want to help you. Is this how you get ideas for new stories?"

Victor chuckled. "I have no ideas of my own. I do what I'm told."

"That's right. I understand that. When you're Victor, you do what you're told. So who can I be?"

"You are who you are, little brother."

"Little brother," the boy repeated, appreciative of his designation. "I always wanted a brother. Where are we?"

"This place belongs to Thomas. He lives upstairs." Victor speared a finger into the darkness overhead. "But that's a secret. No one else knows. The cops have made their search, but ignorant as they are of the netherworld, they found nothing."

"So, Thomas is sort of like your alter ego, too? Victory and Thomas?"

"He dreams the dreams, I carry out the schemes," Victor chanted as he pranced around the chair. He squatted on his haunches like a dog sitting near the boy's feet.

"You were Little Fox, right?" the boy whispered. "In real life?"

"That was Tommy T. Different story."

"I know. Now you're Victor. But I read somewhere that you get your ideas from—"

"Not me." Victor waved the notion away. "I don't get ideas. Victory's always telling me, 'Don't get any ideas, fool.' When I try to think for myself, I usually end up drifting down Shit Creek."

The boy pondered this for a moment.

"So, are you like one of those split-personality people?"

"I'm a changeling." Victor smiled, gratified. "I've changed. I really have. I do important work now. I was nothing before, but now I serve a real purpose."

The boy leaned as far forward as his bonds would permit. "If you took the rest of this tape off, I could serve a purpose, too."

"You already have. You were the key."

"Yeah, and your ally. But I could help with the stories. I wouldn't draw anything that makes you puke, either."

"The only thing that makes me puke is that creek I was telling you about. And running low on medicine."

"Are you a diabetic or something?"

"Something." Victor nodded thoughtfully. "Yeah, something like that. That's why you can't let them lock me up, little brother."

"I don't want anyone to lock you up. I'll tell them you didn't do anything to me. As long as you don't hurt me, it'll be okay."

"I can't let you tell them anything at all, little brother." Victor rose slowly and stood on hind legs, which he could not easily straighten. They ached for the freedom to run, just as his throat ached for the freedom to howl and his head ached to be free from the trouble of thinking.

But for now, some thinking was necessary, and there was one troublesome thought that could not be avoided.

"No, little brother. I can't let you go."

chapter 17

JESSE DIDN'T KNOW WHAT TO MAKE OF Tom's discovery. He had stood guard over Tom's work during the search of his apartment, and he was certain the drawings had not been there the previous day. He had watched Murphy lovingly sort through shelves and file drawers, painstakingly sifting through papers. Now the two of them stood there staring at the old leather portfolio as though it were a set of stone tablets. *Miracle or curse?*

"You didn't see this thing yesterday, did you?" Jesse asked Murphy, just to make certain his own eyes hadn't lied to him.

"It wasn't here. I checked every cubbyhole, Jess, even the trash can. Didn't see anything that looked like that."

"We'll have to bag it and take it back with us," he said, turning to his son. "It'll be examined for prints."

"Mine are all over it."

Jesse rolled his eyes. "Smart move."

"I'm making a lot of them lately," Tom admitted as he sank into a leather chair.

His posture reminded Jesse of the now-gleeful, now-gloomy teenager he had raised. "So how about trying something else?"

"Maybe I need to see a psychiatrist. A hypnotist, maybe. Something's gotta be fuckin' with my head."

"You don't think you did this," Jesse prompted. No question allowed.

"Victor did it." With a gesture, Tom surrendered to the absurd. "I have no doubt, Jesse. There really is a Victor, and he's got Aaron. What I don't know is, whose body is he walking around in?"

"Not yours."

"You don't think so?" A lopsided smile didn't diminish the sadness in Tom's eyes. "I appreciate the confidence. That makes one of us."

Murphy had the kitchen doors and drawers banging in the background. "Yo, Tom, you got any plastic garbage bags?"

"In the pantry, around the corner from the refrigerator."

"Cool," Murphy called out. "Great wine storage. It looks like an old mailbox. Where did you find it?"

"It was here," Tom shouted.

"Shut up about the architecture, Murph. I'm trying to do some business here." Jesse slid a stool up next to Tom's chair and straddled it, getting into detective mode. Or father mode. One sometimes slopped over into the other. "You've gotta level with me, Tom. Have you seen Stony since his release?"

"Don't even go there, Jesse." Sadness turned to stormy scowl. "Don't try to drag my brother into this mess. There's a reason why he doesn't want me to know where he is."

"And I'm that reason," Jesse concluded.

"Maybe *I'm* the reason. Who the hell knows anymore? He used to look after me a lot when I was little, like I was his own kid. 'You don't miss school without a good reason,' he'd say to me. 'Are you sick, Tommy T? You got a fever? I'll get you something for it if I have to steal it, but you don't miss school.' Hell, he'd already quit school a long time ago, but he always said I was the smart one."

"He was right about some things," Jesse said quietly.

"Somewhere along the way, it seemed like I passed him up. I felt like the older one. My big brother was goin' stupid on me."

Jesse nodded.

"Yeah, I know, you told me so."

"I don't think so, Tom. I didn't have to."

"You should have stopped him, Jesse. You'd'a never let me get away with the lies he told to cover up for what he was doing to himself."

"No question, Tom, you'd'a never let *yourself* get by doing drugs. As for Stony, obviously he didn't get away with it. But if it had been up to you, he would have. And I don't mean that in a bad way."

"Is there a good way?"

"He was so deep into that shit, he didn't want to get away. Or maybe he couldn't. All I know is, there comes a time when you have to let go. Stony was bound to do what he was going to do, and he wasn't about to let anyone stand in his way." Jesse forestalled any disagreement by raising two fingers. "And without a way to stop him, if it had been up to you, he would have gotten away with it. Somehow the shit he was doing would have been good for him."

"I don't live in a fairy tale, Jesse. I might work in one, but that's not the way I live."

"I wish I did," Murphy put in. "Drive around in the Supercar, stop bullets with your bare hand, save the world before nightfall, just in time to climb into bed with somebody who looks like Halle Barry." The object of two startled stares, Murphy shrugged and gave an apologetic smile as he unfolded a large green plastic bag. "You talk about a good way, man, that is *it*."

"You asked me to bring him," Jesse reminded his son with a sigh. "I made some calls, Tom. I paid a visit to the warden at Stillwater, who told me that Stony had become quite a reader during his time in prison. When he left, he donated his entire Thomas Warrior collection to the prison library."

"I sent him those. He never asked for anything, and I never knew whether he got anything I sent." He glanced away, adding quietly, "Maybe it looked like I was trying to show him up with all my accomplishments."

"Then I called Stony's parole officer," Jesse continued. "I'd say Stony drew himself an asshole in the parole officer lottery. Said Stony went back to the rez, where the state couldn't touch him. 'Same old story,' was what he said. Made it sound like that's what all Indians do, you know, hightail it back to the reservation. He wasn't looking me in the face, mind you, and I don't know whether he heard me tell him my name was Brown

Wolf." Jesse gave a dry chuckle. "I just let it go and put in a call to Standing Rock Law and Order. Had a friend check around. Nobody's seen Stony in several months."

"So he did go back to South Dakota?"

"Apparently."

"That's more than I knew before. He's probably okay, then."

"Did you hear the part about *nobody's seen him in months?* Tom," Jesse said, again taking an instructive tone, "remember when Stony stayed with us, how we used to tease him about hoarding food in his closet?"

"*You* teased him," Tom clarified. "Myself, I didn't think it was too funny."

"Remember his favorite?"

"Spam." Tom smiled, remembrance bringing a gleam to his eyes. "Yeah, I did tease him about that."

"What's wrong with Spam?" Murphy wanted to know. "That's your key to a good ol' Minnesota hot dish right there. Four cans and a casserole dish and you're set for the church potluck. You've got your canned meat, canned soup, canned mixed vegetables, canned . . ." Ticking them off, he stalled on the fourth finger. "What's the fourth can?"

"I found it on the floor downstairs," Jesse told Tom.

"What was it?"

"Not your goddamn recipe, Murphy. I stepped on a piece of Spam. I'd know that smell anywhere."

Tom's glance ricocheted from cop to cop. "Is this what passes for detective work these days?"

"Who do you think brought this gift?" Jesse pointed to Tom's drawing table, where Murphy was wrapping the old portfolio in plastic, using a dishtowel to protect any evidence that might be found on it.

"No," Tom warned softly.

"Stony's been—"

"No!"

"You didn't know. I don't doubt that. But he's been here, Tom."

"Why wouldn't I know?"

"How long has it been since you were down on the second or third floor?"

Tom shrugged. "I haven't had any reason to go down there in the last, I don't know, six months maybe."

"Well, somebody opened a can of Spam down there."

"Not Stony. He could've stayed up here with me. He knew that. As long as he . . ." Again, Tom glanced away, his voice dropping to a whisper. ". . . stayed clean."

"If he got into your apartment to leave those drawings for you, he could've gotten in to use your computer."

"Then where's Aaron?" Tom demanded. After a brief staring match, he gave the ultimate challenge, the one they'd both been holding off, using all their strength to keep it from bursting through the closet door. "You think Stony killed him?"

"I hope not, but that's the way it usually goes."

"The way it *usually* goes? You're talking about Stony Little Warrior. He wouldn't hurt a fly. He would never hurt anybody, Jesse. You know that."

"Nobody but himself," Jesse acknowledged. "Until—"

"Maybe I'm in on it with him."

Calmly refusing to bite, Jesse shook his head. "If you

were, why would you call me?"

"Why wouldn't I? Wouldn't that throw you off?"

"You don't want to throw me off, Tom," Jesse claimed quietly, his rational tone a counterpoint to Tom's emotional one. "You want me to find Aaron."

Tom sprang out of the chair. "That's right, Dog, that's your job. So stop barking up the wrong tree."

"Is there something we might have missed downstairs?"

"If you saw two floors full of junk, you got the picture," Tom said, heading for the door. "But let's go take another look. Maybe he'll invite us to supper."

THE SECOND SEARCH HAD TURNED UP LESS than the first one. The three men were stymied. Tom asked if he could return the precious ledger drawings to Cassandra after they were dusted for fingerprints, but Murphy assured him that she would get them back eventually. There was more to the process than looking for prints these days.

Jesse suggested that they check out any of the old haunts that Tom might recall from the days when he'd lived on the streets. Murphy took the portfolio to the precinct, while Jesse rode with Tom on what they both knew to be a fool's journey. It had been more than fifteen years. They were not going to find Stony Little Warrior hanging out in the old squats and talking old times with people they had known way back when, most of whom, young or old, were probably dead now. But they made the rounds anyway.

One of the highway overpasses—Tom remembered it as having been pretty secure from a squatter's perspective—had been rerouted, rehabbed, and repurposed. A few blocks away, a drainage ditch had been fenced off. Tom's favorite church with the sheltered basement entry had been torn down. Near an ever-under-construction inner-city highway, an immigrant family had taken refuge in the cozy culvert where he and Stony had slept whenever they'd managed to get there first. Tom had no idea where the four adults and three children had come from or what language they were speaking—no doubt trying to explain to the two Native Americans who had taken them by surprise that they were only trying to get out of the wind while they ate their meal, which Tom pretended not to notice. It was grocery store produce, past its prime.

He allayed their fears by pressing all the cash he had in his pocket into the palm of each hand he shook. "Good luck," he said. "Take care of the little ones."

Jesse hung back, fully aware that he was covered with the smell of cop. His presence would scare the bejesus out of these people, who were probably illegal, possibly employed, likely unable to pay rent. But today their status was not his concern. Nor was the mental condition of the man he and Tom had questioned in the alley behind the café where Angela had once worked, nor the "profession" of the woman on the street corner who looked like someone Tom thought Stony used to get high with. Jesse had only one concern today, and that was the whereabouts of one ex-con and one kid.

But he was proud of his son. Jesse empathized with Tom's fresh and frightening doubts. The young man had begun to think he might be losing his mind. Plagued with that kind of doubt, a lesser man could lose himself entirely. Jesse had been there, and he knew what it felt like to wonder who he really was. Full-blown identity crisis. It was worse than the first time around—when it was just something you had going on like everybody else, the kid trying to find himself—because then you'd been looking for something you never had. It was far worse to lose the man you'd worked hard to become. In an instant, a tragic turn of events could turn a fully functional, self-confident man into a worthless piece of garbage. The death of a child could surely do a man in, especially when that man had been the unwitting—or witless—cause.

But Tom was hanging in there, even though the strain was beginning to show in his face. At the end of the day, Tom hoped to find the boy alive. No Stony, no Victor, no psych ward for himself. But he was willing to risk those dreaded discoveries. Finding the boy was all that mattered.

Jesse laid a hand on his son's back as they climbed the steep embankment from the culvert to the roadside, where Jesse had parked his car.

"You feel sick, too?" Tom asked.

"Yeah," Jesse said. "I'll try to find them a place."

"They'll be gone when you come back."

"Probably."

"It's hard when you know winter's coming."

chapter 18

JESSE DROVE AWAY, LEAVING TOM STAND-
ing in the parking lot behind his building with keys in
hand and a bad case of the blues. He bounced the keys in
his palm. The house key wasn't speaking to him the way
the car key was. Damn, he had it bad for that woman.

He wondered whether a guy could "have it bad" in a
good way.

If the guy was half black and half Lakota, why not?

He rang the doorbell and worked on his cool while he
waited on her front steps. He had good reason to be
there, news he wanted to be the first to tell her.

"Your ledger drawings have been recovered," he
announced as he stepped inside.

"The police called and said they had good news. I
thought it was about Aaron." She closed the door and
turned to him, her eyes nearly colorless, devoid of feeling. "It was only the drawings."

"Did they tell you where they were?"

"I guess I didn't ask. I jumped down the man's throat
about calling me with the wrong good news and told
him to burn the damn drawings." Her lower lip trembled, betraying the effort it took for her to meet his gaze
without shedding tears. "There must be something we
can do, Thomas. I have a feeling *they're* looking for a
body at this point instead of a boy, while *we* know he's
alive. We're sure of that, aren't we?"

"We're optimistic."

"Why are you hedging? You said you see him alive.

You told me that. If you see him alive, then you're *certain* he's *alive*."

"I'm . . ."

She grabbed his arms above his elbows and tried to shake him. But he was unshakable.

"I need to hear you say it, Thomas."

"What difference does it make what I say? I don't see him here." He glanced past her, scanning the dining room. "I'm not seeing him sitting at that table. I'm seeing him in here." With one long finger, he tapped his temple. "You know what else is up here, Cassandra? Cartoons."

"What's wrong? There's something you're not telling me." Her hand slowly slid down his arm. "I'm sorry. I haven't given you much of a chance, have I?"

"I wish I could be sure they were only cartoons. Right now I'm not sure of anything." He squeezed her hand when it finally dropped into his. "Don't ask me what's up, baby. Somebody says *'What's happening,'* I gotta say 'You tell me.'" He glanced at the chandelier in the foyer. "I wish I knew for sure that they were only cartoons."

"You're scaring me again."

With his mind full of worries, hers barely registered. "I wish I had kept them inside my head. I should've never turned them loose."

"Thomas, none of this is your fault."

"I don't know about that, but it doesn't matter anymore. What matters is that the guy who took Aaron has to be the same guy who took the drawings. Which I found on my drawing board when I got home this morning."

She stared at him, bemused. "That's where they

found them?"

"That's right, baby, you laughed before you heard the big punch line. I found the drawings and turned them over to the cops. There they were when I got home this morning, the whole portfolio sitting right there on my desk, just as pretty as you please." He waited for a word, a change in the expression on her face, some sign. But he saw none. "You believe that?" he asked quietly.

"It's pretty incredible, but of course I believe it."

"Anyway, that's the way I remember it. I called Jesse."

"What did he say?"

"He said it was pretty incredible. So we're all in agreement on that point." He took her hand, sat on the deacon's bench, and drew her down beside him.

"Cassandra, in my stories, Victor is the trickster hero. He's a changeling. You know what that means?"

"Exactly what it sounds like. He changes form."

"Right. His body changes, so we call him a shape-shifter. But maybe that's not the way it really works. Maybe he shifts minds." He leaned close, touching his forehead to hers. "Like he'd be me for a while—or I'd be him, however you want to look at it—and then he'd move out of my head into yours, and he'd be you."

"That's not the way you wrote it, so I don't see how it can work that way."

"I didn't create the Trickster." He closed his eyes. Lulled by the cool feel of her skin, he whispered, "He's as old as the ground underneath this house."

"All right." She drew back, taking his pillow away, jerking him up. "What if he does play musical heads?"

He laughed. At every turn she was there at his side, come Coyote or high water.

"Maybe I could lock Victor back up in the closet and start writing psychology books, huh? I could be Thomas Little Freud." He had to think that one over. "Except that I have too many names already. Maybe I've been too many people."

"Please stop this." She laid her soft hand on his cheek, plied his face with her soft eyes. "I'm in love with you, Thomas. You know that, don't you?"

"You make it sound like a threat. *I'm in love with you, so you damn well better behave yourself.*" He smiled. "I know what you're saying. But you love Aaron, too. And we have to find him, Cassandra. No matter what."

"No matter what?"

"You might be a little crazy—love will do that to you—but you're a woman who never ignores the truth. No matter what it costs."

"Not if I—"

"You know how they say follow the money? We've got no money to follow here. We've got to follow the drawings."

"That sounds reasonable," she said, nodding. "Should we go to the police station?"

"No. The police are busy dusting them up, taking X-rays, trying to get blood out of the old leather and all like that. But that's not the way you get them to talk to you."

"They've spoken to you of their own accord," she recalled with a smile.

"That's right." He kissed her hand as he rose from the bench. It felt like the suave thing to do before he took off in search of gremlins and *gigi* men. "Absolutely right. I don't even have to be in the same room with them."

"Where are you going?"

"To follow the drawings. Retrace their journey."

"How can you . . ." She started for the coat closet. "I'm going with you."

"Not this time, baby." He turned her away from the closet door and gave her a quick, hard kiss. "You talk too much."

"Thomas!"

"Not that I don't love the sound of your voice, but that's the problem. I need to listen for the voices in my head." He gave another kiss, more lingering, meant to settle her into his thinking. "It's all about perspective, Cassandra. You need to keep yours, for Aaron's sake. And I need to find mine."

Perspective?

Cassandra scowled as he disappeared by putting the front door solidly between them. He'd been saying *we*—we have to find him; we have to follow the drawings—right up until he walked out and put her right back in the *I* column. What was he talking about, *keep your perspective for Aaron's sake?* She was so confounded she didn't know which way was up.

No, it was worse than that. She was in so deep, she didn't even know whether there *was* an up. What kind of perspective did that leave her with? She was in love with a man whose head was full of talking drawings, the man whom the police suspected of kidnapping her nephew.

"Oh, my God," she whispered as she drew back the curtain on the sidelight window and watched him bound down the first level of steps in the long front sidewalk as he headed for the car he'd parked in front of her house. "He really is the prime suspect. Maybe the only suspect."

Hearing herself say it didn't convince her that it was true. It didn't change the way simply watching him walk away made her heart thud against the walls of her chest like a kid clamoring to run after him.

Was she becoming one of *those* women, the kind who couldn't see the truth about the man she loved no matter what transgressions he committed?

Not according to Thomas. *No matter what.*

She turned away from the window, pressing her back against the front door. The only evidence she knew about—the computer messages and the stolen drawings—pointed to Thomas. And he'd done nothing to hide it.

"Oh, my *God,*" she whispered again before covering her mouth with trembling fingers.

Thomas was his own prime suspect.

"Where are you going, Thomas?" she whispered to the front door. "Do you know?"

He didn't know, but Victor did. She was sure of that now. Was it possible that they were one and the same?

It's all about perspective, Cassandra.

She grabbed her car keys and flew to the back door.

HE DIDN'T KNOW WHERE TO GO TO FIND HIS other half—God help him, his sick half—but wherever that was, the boy was there, too. And he was alive. He had to be.

He drove the route he had taken with Jesse, starting at the place where they'd walked away from the culvert dwellers and working backward. He knew damn well he was jabbing in the dark, but doing the whole thing in reverse seemed strangely logical. Maybe he was taking the part of a Lakota *heyoka,* the contrary who did every-thing backward. It was better than being a trickster, he decided. One way to unravel a huge tangle was to follow the string in reverse. It might not be the best way, but it was all he could think of.

Don't be fooled by the man who says his way is best. How does he know? Is he God? If you try to think about doing whatever you do in a good way, then in the end you'll know you've done your best.

"Victory?"

Victory? He was talking to a cartoon character. He wasn't sitting at his desk drawing pictures. He was driving around town having a conversation with an imaginary friend. Jesus, he *was* crazy.

You're going home, Thomas. You can drive around town all you want, but you know where you'll end up.

"Back at the drawing board, where I found the draw-ings."

They were a gift, Thomas. Now, who would give you such a gift?

"Cassandra."

They are not hers to give.

"She bought them."

Money can't buy those drawings. They're priceless.

Now try again, Thomas. Who could give you such a gift?

"They sure as hell don't belong to Victor."

Why not? He's Lakota. They belong to all of us.

"I don't want the drawings. I want the boy."

We want the drawings, Thomas. We want them for our children because they tell our story, and they tell it our way. It's all in the—

"Perspective. Yeah, I know." He laughed out loud as he made a right turn on red. "I can't believe I just interrupted one of my own damn voices. You know where he is, don't you, Victory?"

If I know, then you also know.

"Shit." He wasn't like Cassandra. If the price was going to be too high, he didn't want to hear the truth. He sighed. "What do I have to do?"

You'll have to let Victor go.

"Is that all?" He laughed. "Hell, take him. There's a hundred more where he came from."

More than that. Much more than a hundred. But for you, there's only one, and he's ready to move on.

"Like I said, take him."

He pulled into the alley and parked behind his building. "This is where they ended up."

That's right.

"They were here all along, weren't they? The ledger drawings. Victor." He dragged his gaze up one, two, three, four floors as he got out of the car and closed the door. "And Aaron."

A classy white car cruised into the alley. Cassandra.

"You followed me."

Squinting against the autumn sun, she closed the car

door behind her.

"Wasn't I supposed to? If you're on the verge of an epiphany, I'm going to be there when it happens."

"An epiphany? Isn't that a religious experience? I think what I'm having is more like a psychotic episode." He put his arm around her when she reached his side. She'd done what she was supposed to. He needed a witness. "Are you a religious person, Cassandra? That's something I don't know about you."

"I think so. I believe in God, if that's what you mean." She looked up at the painted windows, the mysterious part of the building. "I don't think I believe in devils and demons, though." She glanced at him. "I'm not so sure about changelings, either."

"Good. Hang on to those doubts. I need that objective eye."

"What are you going to do?"

"What I do best," he told her as he led the way through the side door. "We'll see what happens." And then he added, "But don't talk."

elsewhere

"I BUNGLED THE MISSION WHEN I BROUGHT you here," Victor whispered to his protégé.

"Maybe we can fix it," the boy said through a mouthful of bread and canned meat. He wasn't turning his nose up at Victor's food anymore.

In the past few days Victor hadn't been able to stomach much more than the smell, which reminded him of another life with another little brother. Rather than flashing before his eyes, his life seemed to be plodding through all of his senses lately. Mostly smell. He'd surely had some high-smellin' times.

The boy was taped to his chair by only one arm. As long as his new little brother didn't try to do anything foolish, Victor had decided to loosen up on him, limb by limb. Victor knelt beside the chair, chewing on the bit of thumbnail he'd overlooked in the first pass he'd made on his right hand.

"We lost the treasure. It's turning out just like Victory said it would." Victor spat the bit of nail into the dark. "She's always right. She said they would come looking for you, and that's how they got the treasure back."

"Why do you say *treasure?*" The boy wiped his mouth on the side of his hand. "They're just old drawings. I think what we need to do is to go after some real treasure, like gold or jewels."

"Thomas decides what the mission will be." With a gloomy sigh, Victor rested chin on fist and fist on Little Brother's taped arm. "But you and me, we're finished now. He won't give me any more work to do. Just when you're almost ready to give me a hand."

"Why not?"

"Because they're watching him now." Victor stood abruptly and began padding back and forth on bare feet. "What am I going to do with you, little brother? What, what, what?"

"Let me talk to them," the boy pleaded, and not for the first time. "Let me tell them it's okay. I'm your ally."

"You would do that, wouldn't you?"

"Yes!"

"And you really think that would keep them from locking us up."

"Well . . ." The boy paused, assessing the wisdom of coming right out with it. "They're not gonna lock me up anyway, Victor. I'm the kid they think you napped."

"Nabbed," Victor corrected. He'd picked a good one to nab, he told himself. Honest and gutsy. "The truth is, I did nab you. They'll give me life, and that's only because this isn't a death penalty state."

"We're playing a game. We're, like, role-playing. I've always wanted to get into a role-playing game. You're the first one who's ever invited me."

"You've been an excellent guest. But now, I don't know. I have to think of something on my own."

"Let's ask Thomas."

"We can't do that." Victor gave it a moment's thought—if there was any way—but finally he shook his head. "No, we totally can't do that. Thomas only imagines me, you know."

"That's what I thought I was doing at first, but you're real." The boy looked up toward a ceiling he couldn't see. "I mean, this is a real building somewhere, and I'm really taped to this chair, and you're real."

"I'm afraid you're right. I'm a real fuckup."

"I didn't say *that*."

"If I had it to do over again, I'd be more like you, little brother. You're the smart one. You learn fast. You hang in there, make the best of a bad situation, don't smoke, drink, or cuss. And you're an excellent guest."

The boy looked flabbergasted. "You'd wanna be like me?"

"I would." Squatting on his haunches in front of the chair, Victor gave an open-handed gesture. "You see what happens when I think for myself? This is what happens. Now I'll have to figure out what to do, and my head hurts too much to do any figuring."

"You can't kill me," the boy said, all sensible and matter-of-fact.

"Why can't I?"

"What would you do with my body? It's just about impossible to dispose of a body without getting caught. And even if you did get rid of me without leaving the slightest little trace, well, they'd keep coming back to Thomas." Another pause. "Don't you think?"

"No." Victor braced his elbows on his knees and held his increasingly sick head in his hands. "No, I don't think."

"Maybe you should take your medicine, Victor. You're shaking. Do you have any medicine?"

"I've been saving up." Victor sprang to his feet and took Little Brother's suggestion for a bona fide medical recommendation. Permission from the smart one. With tattered duffel bag in hand, Victor sat on the floor at the edge of the circular beam created by his flashlight.

"You know what I did, little brother?" Victor asked excitedly. "The last time I hooked up with the medicine man, he left me alone in the back of the van, just for a few minutes—he thought I was totally wasted, you know, but I wasn't—and I helped myself to his stash while he wasn't looking. Not so much that he'd notice, but enough so I'd have a little extra for a rainy day. And I've kept it safe all this time. Safe from myself, mostly." In the shadows he arranged his hoard, all nicely bundled in plastic. "Whatcha think? Pretty good, huh?"

"With your, um, illness, I think it's good to always have medication on hand," the boy acknowledged tentatively.

"Always thinking, my little brother, but that's okay for a guy like you." Victor reached into the duffel bag for pencil and paper. He tore several scribbled-up pages from the pad and cast them aside. He never could draw worth a damn. But he was pretty sure he could write, even with his hands shaking.

"I'm gonna give you a mission," he told the boy.

"Really?"

"You'll have to leave this place, the only place where we're safe, and you'll have to go up there." With the pencil, Victor pointed to a small door behind the big chair. "It's a steep and narrow path, dark all the way. The best thing is to just keep going and not think about anything else. Just run up the stairs and don't look back."

"What's at the top of the stairs?"

"A secret door, of course. A secret place always has a secret door."

"What's my mission?"

"Have a little patience, brother. I want you to tell Thomas that he can take the rest of the treasures to the people now. All the stuff I've liberated; it's all here, inside this chest." He tapped the end of the pencil on the wooden crate behind his shoulder. "You tell Thomas and no one else. Is that understood?"

"Y-yes. I guess."

"You're not going to fail in this, are you, little brother?" Victor asked, returning to his writing.

"No. I'm going to tell Thomas and nobody else."

"There's one more thing. Do you know Thomas's father, Jesse Brown Wolf?"

"The policeman?"

"That's the one." Victor tore his letter off the pad and folded it in half. "Give him this. I've never done this before, but maybe it'll help me cross over in a good way. A little bit, anyway. Ask Jesse to sing for me. That's important, now, don't forget."

"Tell Jesse to sing for you," the boy repeated solemnly.

"He'll know."

"You're shaking really bad. You'd better get that medicine in you."

"My little brother is looking after me." Victor tried to smile, but his face felt numb, so he couldn't tell whether it was happening. He reached behind the duffel bag, patted around on the floor with an unsteady hand.

"You want me to help?"

"No!" He could have used the help, but not from the boy. He waved him on. "It's time for you to take off. Right through there. It's a spiral stairs. Keep one hand on the pole, and don't be scared. Hurry, little brother. Don't think about anything but getting up those stairs."

Aaron tucked Victor's message into the back of his pants, where the waistband had some give. He pictured himself looking super cool when it was time to whip that message out and hand it over.

He wasn't sure what a spiral stairs was, and Victor was right about the shaft behind the secret door being a scary place. Aaron's eyes had gotten used to figuring out shapes in near darkness, but his body had been glued to the chair for such a long time that it didn't want to loosen up and step out.

From several feet away, Victor's flashlight illuminated a couple of metal steps, which were wrapped around the pole Aaron had been told to hold on to. But the treads were so tiny! He had to stick close to the pole or slip off the edge of the steps into a black hole, never to be seen again.

With a one-handed death grip on the pole, he reached out to see if he could touch the wall of the shaft. His fingers found bricks. Dirt and bugs, too, probably, but he'd never know unless something bit him.

·Being totally in the dark wasn't all bad.

Taking quick measure of the width of the steps with his feet and the extent of the shaft with his outstretched arm, Aaron figured that he couldn't fall between the steps and the wall.

Being totally fat wasn't all bad.

Now, if he only knew where he was going and how many steps it would take him to get there. He started up the stairs, using the toe of his shoe to find its next perch as he listened for any sound other than the pounding of his own heart. He felt like Jack, but he was trying to make it up the beanstalk indoors and in the dark. He didn't know what he'd run into at the top, but at this point a giant would seem like no big deal.

His progress was way too slow for a man on a mission. He needed that flashlight. Afraid to turn around, he retraced his steps, carefully backing down the shaft.

"Victor, can I use . . ."

Aaron's rubber soles squealed on the wood floor. Victor had flopped over to one side like a rag doll. He hadn't even put his shot needle and diabetic stuff away. The coyote skin covered his face.

"Victor?" The boy knelt beside the spent shell of the man who had lured him to the park, tossed a blanket over his head, and brought him to this place. Aaron gently shook his shoulder. "Victor, what's wrong? Can you wake up?" He shook again. "Did you take too much medicine, Victor? Can I just see your . . ."

He lifted the animal skin for his first real peek at Victor's face. It was streaked with black and reddish paint, somehow familiar, but not exactly the face Aaron had imagined it might be.

No movement, no sound, no recognition on either side. "I gotta get you some help."

Aaron snatched up the flashlight and headed back up the spiral stairs, his ascent fueled by an extra shot of fear. When the beam of light finally landed on something that looked like a door, he started calling for help. Someone up there was calling his name. Two voices.

"Aaron, are you all right?"

"Something's holding the door from that side," a deep voice said. "Can you release it?"

Aaron took the wooden bar off its iron hooks, stepped back, and pulled on the handle. The heavy piece of wood fell from his hand and clattered down the shaft. It was still falling when two faces appeared in the frame of light at the top of the stairs.

"Aunt Cassie?"

"Aaron!"

"We have to call a doctor for Victor. I don't think he's breathing."

chapter 19

TOM STOOD BACK IN AMAZEMENT. THE WALL of cubby holes that he'd used as a perfect wine rack—he'd assumed it had once been an office mail center or storage—actually swung open, exposing an opening in the wall.

Cassandra grabbed Aaron and nearly took his head off dragging him through the half-sized doorway. She was chattering tearfully. Aaron was blubbering breathlessly. Tom didn't understand any of it except that the boy was alive. *Reborn,* was Tom's first celebratory thought.

But when Aaron saw Tom, the confusion tripled.

"It's you!" The boy's weary eyes widened. He was overjoyed. "I knew you weren't him, but sometimes I wasn't totally sure, because who else could he be?"

"Where is he, Aaron?"

The child pointed to the opening he'd just burst through.

"Those little stairs wrap around a pole. He's *way* down there. But I think he took too much of his diabetes medicine, because I tried really hard, and I couldn't wake him up."

Tom beamed the light down the shaft, then up toward the roof. Oddly, the shaft of light appeared to dissolve, but the circle of light at the top remained bright. It became a perfectly round, white orb drifting toward the roof of the building.

A warm, joyous rush passed through Tom's body, even though the stairwell was decidedly chilly. He turned the flashlight off, but the white beam remained for an instant—a pure, simple, harmless bubble, finally free to float where it would.

One of those dots you see in the dark after the lights go out, Tom told himself as he thrust the flashlight into the closest hand. "Hand me this after I get myself in here."

"Should I come down?" Aaron asked, following Tom's order. "I'm his ally. He might be scared if he sees you."

"I don't think so."

"But you might not be able to see him," Aaron called out from above. Tom was working his way down. "You only just imagine him. I can really *see* him. I'm his ally."

"Stay with Aunt Cassie. I'll let you know what we need."

Tom saw the bare feet first, both tipped to one side in still repose. He focused the light on those heart-wrenchingly dirty soles. The light would hurt his eyes. Just like with Dark Dog. He hated the light. Tom's deepest hope was for the pain to be gone. No more pain.

He knelt beside the pile of rags—mostly black and gray, his own design—a makeshift costume assembled from baggy pants, voluminous tunic, and coyote pelts.

Except for the feet, it was hard to imagine that a human form lay somewhere underneath it all.

But he did. Tom had outstripped his big brother's height when he was fifteen, but the difference in their stature was unnatural. The body swaddled in rags was barely there. Tom brushed the matted hair back from his brother's painted face. His eyes were open, but there was no life in them. Tom felt for a pulse anyway, knowing he would find nothing but the feel of cool skin stretched over protruding bones. But for the night sky black and earth red paint, the face might have vanished for lack of substance.

"A man can't live on Spam alone," Tom whispered huskily, words he had said more than once with a teasing grin on his face.

A call came from on high.

"Thomas, can I come down now?"

"Call 911," Tom shouted back. "Tell them it's an overdose."

"But can I come down?"

"No!"

"I'm his ally! He calls me—"

Tom could hear Cassandra talking to the boy.

"But he calls me Little Brother," Aaron insisted loudly.

More talking. Tom couldn't hear what she was saying, but he recognized that comforting tone. She knew what he needed, what Aaron needed, how to do right by both of them.

"Should we let the boy say good-bye, Stony?" Tom whispered, his throat clotted with sadness. "Or is it Victor now? My brother either way."

"They're on their way, Thomas." The welcome sound of Cassandra's voice echoed in the stairwell. "Is there any other way they can get in down there?"

"I don't see any. Ask Aaron."

"I never could see very well down there, Thomas," Aaron shouted. "We could hear the police searching for me one time, but they never found anything. I don't know how he gets in and out, except for the spiral stairs."

"There's only straight up, right, bro?" Tom whispered. "So you like my stories, huh? I'm glad. I wish . . ." He wiped his dripping nose on his cuff. Stony would have reprimanded him for messing up his shirt. Then, without thinking, he would have done the same thing. Tom smiled through his tears. "I'm sorry I didn't do better by you. I should have . . . I should have . . ."

Somebody was singing a church song. Aaron.

"Stop it," Thomas said, then turned toward the stairs. "Stop it!"

"He said it was important to sing for him," Aaron shouted. "He wanted Jesse to do it, but Jesse isn't here yet."

"Did you call him?"

"I called him, Thomas." Cassandra—bless her—understood that shouting was unnecessary. "Do you know who he is?"

"He's our brother. Mine and Aaron's. Let Aaron come down so we can send our brother over in a good way," he called back. "There's a flashlight in the kitchen drawer under the coffeepot."

Soon he heard the sound of Aaron's footsteps. A hurried descent. A slight slip and a catch. "Ouch!"

"You okay?"

"I'm good. I'm turning around so I can back down, but I'm good. I finally got to use a real bathroom."

"I'll bet that was a relief."

A beam of light announced Aaron's arrival.

"Are you really okay?" Tom asked gently as the boy knelt beside him.

"Victor didn't hurt me a bit, Thomas. Not one bit."

"His name used to be Stony Little Warrior. The old ones tell us not to say a person's name aloud after he's gone, but I want you to know."

"Is he dead?" Aaron reached out, but all he dared touch was the fur pelt. "He told me he was a changeling."

"He told you the truth. If ever two people lived inside one body, it had to be this one."

"Which one is he now?"

"Neither, maybe." Tom lifted his elbow and turned his damp face into his shoulder, trying to get it dry. "Or both. I think he's on his way to being all new."

"Your name's Little Warrior, too?"

"I changed it to make life easier for myself."

"Yeah. I hate Farmer, too." The boy petted the fur fondly. "I think he's been down here for quite a while."

"I didn't know," Tom said sadly. "I guess we'll never know how he discovered all this."

"Secret places always have secret doors and secret stairways. He said to tell you that the rest of the treasure is inside that box. I mean, *chest*. He said you should take it back to the people."

Tom gave in and wept. Aaron turned to hug him, and Tom enveloped the boy in his arms and simply hung on.

"He only took me so he could get the key to Aunt Cassie's house," Aaron said quietly when Tom loosened his hold. "He didn't want to hurt anybody. He wanted to recover all the treasure. That was his mission. The mission you gave Victor. It sounds kind of . . ."

"Crazy?" Tom laughed as he rubbed his face.

"You wanna know what's crazy? I sort of halfways thought he was you."

"I sort of halfways thought so, too. Maybe that's why I failed him. I thought it was all about me."

"You didn't fail him. He said you gave him a purpose. I think he liked being Victor."

Tom nodded.

Another call came from above.

"Tom?"

"Take it easy coming down those steps, Jesse." He blotted his nose on his other cuff. "Oh, God, I don't want him to see me acting like a big kid."

"He's your dad. I bet he's seen you act like one before."

Tom laughed. "Man, you've got that right."

Jesse entered the scene with a third beam of light.

"You were right," Tom whispered as he pushed off the floor with one hand, rising to his feet as steadily as he could manage.

"I'm so sorry."

"I know. I know. But look who we found." He laid his hands on the boy's shoulders and stood him in front of him. "This is Aaron Farmer. This is the man of the hour, right here."

"Victor told me to give you this." Aaron stepped away, stuck his hand under his sweater, and pulled a piece of paper out of the back of his pants. He handed it to Jesse. "And he said to ask you to sing for him. He said it was real important."

Jesse nodded, glancing at Tom. "You remember?"

Jesse took the lead, started the song in a low register, and then lifted it high as Tom joined in. Tom cued the boy with a hand on his shoulder, and Aaron took to the nasal tone naturally, singing from the heart. In near darkness, tears rolled down all three faces.

Low to high, earth to sky, their song let the spirits know that someone they loved was coming.

chapter 20

AARON'S ORDEAL WAS NOT OVER. DESPITE his protests, he would not be spared the inevitable medical and law enforcement examinations. An ambulance awaited.

"Your mom will be waiting for us at the hospital," Cassandra assured him. She had called Darcy with the news that Aaron was safe and explained the procedure as it had been explained to her. The police would have to ask him some questions, but they would be considerate of the ordeal he'd been through.

"But I'm not hurt," Aaron protested for the hundredth time. "Can't I go downstairs and see where I was and where we were hiding when the police searched? There was like this part that I just thought was a big crate, but Victor opened it up somehow, and the stairs were inside there. But it was always dark."

With a glance, Cassandra invited Thomas's support. He needed something to think about besides the noise from the saw and the sledgehammer the firefighters were using downstairs to tear into the false wall so that they could remove the body. Thomas had theorized that his brother had secretly come looking for shelter and had found the perfect hiding place.

"Listen up, my man." Thomas laid a hand on the boy's shoulder. "You take a ride in the ambulance. You record every minute in that artist's memory of yours. You'll use it someday. Experience is one of the things separates guys like us from the hacks."

"I know what he did wasn't right, but I swear he didn't hurt me."

Thomas's hand strayed into Aaron's hair, and Cassandra saw the urge in him to hug the boy, but he turned his head away, his hand floundering as though it had been cut loose somewhere between mussing the hair and patting the shoulder. "I'm sorry, Aaron," he said, his voice husky with emotion.

Aaron wrapped his arms around Thomas's waist. "It wasn't your fault."

"Did he tell you why?"

"I think he wanted to be a hero, kind of. He wanted to make your stories really happen. But you know what?" Aaron looked up. "He really thought he was Victor. And I thought . . . maybe he could be."

Thomas nodded. "I'm going with him now, and Aunt Cassie's going with you. They're going to ask you about everything that happened. You tell it all just like it was." He glanced at Cassandra. "Later, when you feel like it, I want you to tell me."

"I will." Aaron backed away. "But I don't know why I have to see a doctor. All I need is some of my mom's spaghetti."

"Be sure you tell her that when we get to the hospital." Cassandra glanced over her shoulder and read the range of emotions in Thomas's eyes as she led Aaron away. "Maybe she'll make enough for all of us."

DARCY WAITED BENEATH THE EMERGENCY Entrance sign. She screamed her son's name the minute the gurney hit the pavement. Cassandra noticed the way Aaron's eyes lit up at the sound of his mother's voice. He told her that the paramedics had offered him a ride on a rolling bed, and he'd thought it would be rude to refuse.

In the hospital lobby, Cassandra waited with Darcy, who looked as dazed and emotionally drained as Cassandra felt.

"He says he's fine, but he looks different. Older, maybe." Darcy cupped her hand around her own chin. "In the face, you know? Like a little old man. And thinner." She laughed nervously. "He wants my spaghetti. He's watched me open the cans a hundred times. He knows it's more Hunt's doing than mine."

"He likes the way his mom makes it." She reached for

Darcy's hand. "He's made it sound so good, I'm hungry for some, too."

"You'll come home with us?" Darcy asked eagerly. "I'm scared to know what that man did to him. I can't imagine. I mean, I've had all kinds of nightmares, but I don't think I can stand knowing . . ."

"Yes, you can, Darce. Aaron swears he wasn't hurt, but whatever happened, we have to help him deal with it. We don't want our nightmares to compound his."

"If that creep hadn't been able to kill himself, I would have gladly done it for him."

"I know."

"I don't care whose brother he was."

"I know."

"Are you going to go on seeing him? How do we know they weren't in on it together?"

"I'm willing to leave it up to the police to sort it all out. Once they clear Thomas, which they will, I hope he'll still be part of Aaron's life, and mine." She added softly, "We both love him."

"I don't know, Cassie. It doesn't seem right, the way this went down right under the man's own roof. How could he not know?"

"If you could see the building . . ." Cassandra began, trailing off with the knowledge that there was little sense to be made of any of it right now, except that Aaron had been found. "He's a very brave young man, that son of yours."

"I guess so. He kept reassuring me, while I'm blubbering like a crazy woman." Darcy leaned in like a willow, settling her forehead on Cassandra's shoulder.

Cassandra could smell the coffee on her sister's breath. She could feel her trembling. "I expected the worst, Cassie. Didn't you?"

"I tried not to."

"You were always a believer."

"After this, I'll bet you'll be one, too."

"After this, I know I'll never be the same again." Darcy lifted her head and gave her sister a teary-eyed smile. "The difference could really be for the better."

Cassandra nodded, swallowing against the burning in her throat. "Me too."

JESSE'S RIDE TO THE MORGUE WITH THE boys who had come into his life on the verge of their manhood was spent mostly in silence. For years he had wondered whether he had made any difference. He had lost Tom's trust the day he had given up on Stony—and, yes, he had given him up. If truth were told, he had not been sorry to see the two young men go their separate ways. Only then had he been able to stop worrying that the older one might drag the younger one down.

But taking that last ride with a dead boy was heartbreaking. And he was still a boy. Typical of a drug addict, he had never come of age. A man's body lay strapped to the gurney between Jesse and Tom. But the loss they mourned was that of a boy they'd once known.

They avoided each other's eyes, even as they appreciated each other's presence. The ambulance driver did not sound the siren. There was no need to ignore traffic signals, no hurry, no possibility of saving a life. Jesse awaited Tom's cue.

"I want to take him back home," Tom said finally. "Lay him next to our mother. Will you . . ." Tom cleared the gravel from his throat. "Will you help me carry him, Jess?"

Wordlessly, Jesse reached out, offering his son the strength of his arms.

Wordlessly, Tom clasped his father's hands.

epilogue

FROM THE HOTEL WINDOW, CASSANDRA marveled at the way the prairie's snow blanket glistened in the morning sun. She had never been to the Dakotas— except for the Black Hills once as a child, which didn't count—until they had brought Stony home in the fall. If Thomas hadn't persuaded her to make a personal presentation to the Tribal Council, she would never have thought to pay a winter visit. What a view she would have missed! Here the porcelain blue sky was truly infinite, and the rolling snowscape was unmarred by anything man-made.

The bathroom door opened behind her. Fresh from the shower, Thomas slid his arms around her and nipped her ear.

"How important is it for you to get back to the Cities today?"

The feel of him made her shimmer inside, as though

the sun had found a way to make her bones glisten. His arms were warm and dewy, his hair damp, his breath feathery on the side of her neck. "I was just going to ask you that," she said, suddenly wearing the silly smile of a naked mannequin in a store window.

"If it is, we'd better hit the road. There's a storm coming in. Even if we leave now, it'll be nipping our heels all the way home."

"A storm? Where? The sky is as clear as heaven."

"Is this what heaven looks like?" He turned her to face him. He wore the same smile. "Something like this, huh?" His gaze escaped hers for the window. "God's own colors. I don't know if I could live here after growing up in the Cities. I don't know if I'm man enough."

"Man enough?" Her saucy glance hinted that he was a standout in a bath towel.

"This land is so big and open, and its power is overwhelming. Where would I hide?"

"You mean, from your public? A place like this would be perfect."

"If we wait for that storm to blow in, you'll see what *nowhere to run* really means."

"I don't want to run." She snuggled against his bare chest. "I want you to be stuck with me for twenty-four solid hours. No creeping back to your hideout in the middle of the night."

"Baby, you rocked my world from the first moment I saw you, but don't you be trying to change the way I work. You'd best not be screwing around with my creative genius."

"Oh, but that's exactly what I want to screw around

with, Thomas. I can't get enough of your creativity."

He chuckled. "I've finally found a woman who loves me for my mind."

She looked up at him. *Seriously, now.*

"I didn't sound like the rich benefactor, did I?" she asked. "The patron donating *my* collection to the college."

"You said you were returning the ledger drawings to their rightful heirs."

"And that's the way I feel about it. But did it sound sincere?"

"It did to me. But I'm used to that high-toned manner of yours. I know you deep down. I mean, way deep down, you're easy."

She smacked his butt, which he'd constricted into rock formation in anticipation of the chance to show that he could.

She rewarded him with an "Ouch."

He grinned. "Easy to get along with. You know, easygoing. Sincere as all hell."

"But did I sound like the proverbial pompous hardass, giving my collection of Lakota art and artifacts to the Lakota people?"

"We forgive you," he said solemnly. "We accept. We love you just the way you are."

"Are you speaking for the whole Lakota nation? You sound just as pompous as I did. And maybe just a touch harder assed."

"Let's say we're firm. We persevere. We're a proud people. As for myself, I'm speaking for Thomas Warrior and all his alter egos. We love you."

"I love you, too." She tucked her face into the hollow of his neck. "Or three, or four."

His tone turned solemn. "Stony told Aaron that I had given him a mission, some kind of purpose. The sad thing is, I wasn't even thinking about him. I was doing my own thing, waving my own flag. I didn't give him much of myself."

"No matter what you gave, it wouldn't have been enough as long as he was using."

" 'Whatever you give to the least of my brothers,' " he quoted, but either he didn't know the rest, or he didn't want to take it that far. "I didn't give much. The truth is, I didn't mind it that much that he didn't want to see me when he was in prison. I said I was hurt that he didn't call when he got out, but I don't know if that's even true. I think I was kinda relieved. I never contacted his parole officer. We never had much use for cops, so that's how I played it. Jesse gave him up. But I gave up on him. I was all he had. He had to turn himself into somebody else."

"Thomas, you're making it sound like you were the be-all and end-all in your brother's life." She leaned back, looked him in the eye. "Do you really think you're that powerful?"

"I'm not saying I'm powerful. I'm saying I failed him."

"And he had nothing to say about it? It was all up to you, and you failed?"

"You're playing with me now. My brother was living like a rat in my house, and I didn't even—"

"Know. You didn't know. He didn't want you to know, and he succeeded in keeping it from you. He created his own fantasy—no matter what he based it on, he made it his own—and he lived in that fantasy. Now, that's the bottom line, Thomas. You have to give Stony credit for doing his own thing and making it work, in an odd sort of way." She sighed. "I give him credit for letting Aaron go. It could have been so much worse."

"You think Aaron's going to be okay?"

"His counselor says that he's working through it all much better than she expected. His relationship with Darcy is improving, too." She smacked his butt again, catching him off guard this time. "Now get your pants on so we can go downstairs and join your parents for breakfast."

A blizzard blew in from the west, just as Tom had predicted. It would be another day or two before the four of them would be able to drive back to Minneapolis, but nobody seemed to mind being snowed in. All the comforts of a casino hotel and the pleasure of each other's company were theirs to enjoy. They had survived the fear of a child gone missing and the sadness of Stony's death, but Tom had come full circle in his respect for his adopted father. It was good to share a meal together in a good way.

"I think I've come up with a new superhero, Jess," Tom announced over the third round of coffee refills. "You're gonna love him."

"If I inspired him, would you come up with a better name than Dark Dog? I'm getting pretty tired of that handle." Jesse brandished a fist. "I want something fiery, a name that evokes an image of real power and commands respect."

"I hear you, man, and I've got one for you." Tom slid Angela a conspiratorial wink. "It came to me when I noticed how tough these rez dogs are. No, they are truly a menace. I'm thinkin' my new hero is a retired cop."

"Did I say I was ready to retire?"

"No, but thinking ahead a little bit, I decided it was time for me to come up with a mature hero. A man of the people. A man who knows which puppy to put under the Christmas tree and which one to put in the soup kettle."

"I ain't wearin' no red suit, Tommy T."

"That wouldn't be fitting for a superhero. If you're gonna save little kids and kittens from the vicious pack, you can't be walking around in velvet pants."

"You got that right. It's gotta be a *rez* suit. *Big Indian* emblazoned across the chest." Jesse indicated the placement with a sweep of his hand. "He has superpowers and cool weapons?"

"So far, all he has is a name." Tom flashed the twinkle in his eye for his mother and his woman, cherishing each for her special place in his life.

Then he turned to his father, all smiles. "I'm calling him Dog Catcher."

Center Point Publishing
600 Brooks Road ● PO Box 1
Thorndike ME 04986-0001 USA

(207) 568-3717

US & Canada:
1 800 929-9108